Praise f

"Love this inspirational romantic story! This author has done it again! I love the stories that she weaves while also imparting Christian character, principles and God's Truths."

—ANJOMOM16, AMAZON

"After reading all 9 books of this series, I wish there were 9 more. Excellent characters and wonderful story telling on the part of the author. Each character had their own distinct personalities and hidden secrets. You can't go wrong reading this whole series and I promise you won't regret it."

—KYLENE, AMAZON

"The story that unfolds is equal parts humor, mystery and suspense and ultimately a tender love story between two hurting people with a lot of past issues to resolve. I was totally charmed by McKenzie's vulnerability and willingness to share her deepest hurts with Luke and her ability to draw him out of his shell. Luke's response to her was equally touching, full of understanding, protectiveness and love."

—TRACEY, AMAZON

You Don't Have to be a Star

Montana Fire | Book 9

Susan May Warren

About You Don't Have to be a Star

Former Green Beret Luke Alexander just wants to forget his past and mind his own business in the woods of east Tennessee. And, his park ranger job seems just the solution… until a diva movie star walks into his world looking for someplace to hide. But the Cherokee forest isn't big enough for the both of them, not if you include the trouble MacKenzie has dragged along behind her. And soon she's stirring up his own murky past—one out for revenge. Which trouble will find them first? Is it even possible to outrun your past and start over? Luke and MacKenzie are about to find out…

Chapter One

Just once, MacKenzie would like to take the Oscar walk down Hollywood Boulevard in a pair of holey jeans, a Blue Devil's T-shirt, and a pair of flip-flops.

She pulled her wrap tight around her shoulders as the evening chill found the liberal gaps in her dress and raised gooseflesh. A thousand lights blinked down at her from the Kodak Theater, and exhaust from the parade of limousines maneuvering to the end of the red carpet mixed with the earthy smell from the palm trees lined up like sentries along Hollywood Boulevard. She looked for her driver in the mass of shiny vehicles. *Hurry up, Tony.*

Sure, she liked her silver Christian Louboutin sling-backs and the deep-purple satin gown picked by her stylist from some new Australian designer, but she could do without the ten-pound emerald earrings pulling at her ears. She could especially do without the fact that every flash, every pop of light, meant that some gossip rag had fresh ammunition to litter her shame across the newsstands of America.

No, not *her* shame. After all, she'd just returned from halfway across the world, filming in the back alleys and dregs

1

of Bangkok, in an indie drama that exposed the underbelly of human trafficking. While her husband—no, make that *ex-*husband as of two weeks ago—exposed his heart—and *more*, clearly—to the leading lady in his, yes, Oscar-nominated film.

"MacKenzie Grace!" A red carpet host for *Hollywood Tonight*—what was her name, Twila?—pushed a microphone in her face.

MacKenzie just barely refrained from shoving her away. No, smile. *Smile.* "Twila. You look gorgeous tonight."

"And you should be the one earning an Oscar tonight for your magnanimous smile during his win. How do you feel about your ex-husband being nominated for best actor?"

Twila's question meant that MacKenzie had managed to fool the world with said smile for the eternal five seconds the camera had panned to her while Nils Bruno climbed to the stage to accept his award.It was long enough to drill a hole clean through her, leave her exhausted and raw as she watched Nils accept the award, nod to his *hot new girlfriend*, and cleanly excise from his life the woman who'd believed in him, who'd run lines with him, and who footed the bill for his shiny white teeth.

Now, she added a gracious tone. "The Academy clearly saw his talent."

Talent. Like emptying half her bank account and totaling her Aston Martin. That took real talent. *Smile.*

"So, are you interested in costarring again with him? Now that's he's an Oscar winner?"

Translation: would she co-star with him now that Nils Bruno, aka Robby Brunardo, former car-washing burger flipper from McDonalds, had outshined her on the big screen?

"Nils is an amazing actor. Anyone would be privileged to work with him."

2

If she smiled any harder, she might grind her molars to dust.

He used to wear male-shaping garments under his clothes for his publicity shots! she wanted to scream at the top of her lungs.

But a woman trying to charm Hollywood into backing her recent indie film, the one she hoped would launch her from action-thriller babe to serious actress, probably shouldn't publicly disparage one of America's "sexiest men alive."

She still had his old ratty Converse in a box at home. Maybe she could sell them on eBay, earn some cash to promote her new film, maybe raise some discerning heads in the industry . . .

Oh, who was she kidding? She'd been Hayes O'Brien, 006, international action heroine for so long, directors probably forgot she'd earned a degree in drama at Duke. Or that, for a very short run, she'd even been courted by Broadway.

Then again, maybe everyone had simply weeded through her airbrushed beauty to the truth. She couldn't act her way out of a paper bag.

There went Tommy Nave's nasally sixth-grade voice in her head again. She shivered.

Greg Alexander wrapped his warm arm around her shoulders. "Tony will be here in a minute. He's about five limos back."

She wanted to lean into him, but she hated to encourage the press. They already had her dating at least three actors, two of whom she'd never even met. The last thing she needed was a scandal about dating her agent.

"You're doing great, MacKenzie," Greg said, lifting his hand to wave to—oh it didn't matter. She looked away.

You're doing great.

She managed a wan smile as another flash went off.

3

Watching Nils walk the red carpet—without her—had filleted her insides. Drawing a deep breath actually hurt between her ribs.

Greg lifted his arm and waved Tony to the curb. "Okay, sweetheart, you go home, get changed, and I'll meet you at the Vanity Fair party." He held out his hand to help her into the limo.

She ignored it, let the footman open the door for her, gathered her dress, and slid into the seat. But before Greg could shut the door, she put her hand out to stop it. "I'm not going."

He'd turned away, migrating toward his next client. "What?" He looked as if she might have been speaking Bengali. "Did you say you aren't going?"

MacKenzie pulled off one of her shoes. "I'm tired, I have jet lag, and I'll just be followed around all night with microphones and cameras, gossip magazines wondering if I'm pining after Nils."

She waited for a response, but Greg just stared at her, as if still trying to comprehend her words.

"I just want to go home, soak in a bath, maybe eat some pizza." Or pie. Yes, a creamy—maybe coconut cream, or . . . yes, banana cream!—pie. The closest thing she was going to get to banana puddin' this side of the Mississippi.

Greg finally stirred to life—probably at the thought of her reckless consumption of calories. "Kenzie, hon, you need to schmooze, get some face time with the right people, if you hope to get backers for your film. Tonight is the perfect night to generate some buzz. You've been laying low for—"

"I'll call you later." She pulled the door closed and leaned back, thankful for the silence embedded in the plush seats. Tony, his dark hair slicked back and a silver earring in his left ear, glanced up at her in the rearview mirror.

"Home, Miss Grace?"

"Please."

She watched the crowd wave as her limousine pulled away.

Home. Despite her Malibu digs, *home* was really a tidy double-wide with brown shag carpeting, a weathered pink velour sofa, and an irritable tabby named Boss probably running his claws down her mother's orange polyester drapes. There'd be a bowl of cold grits in the fridge, and possibly a container of store-bought animal crackers on the counter—with the lions missing, of course. And her father slumped asleep in his ripped vinyl recliner waiting for Mama to get off her shift at the rayon factory.

Longing curled through her as they passed the luminous red pagoda of Mann's Chinese theater, lit up for the Academy Awards and, across the street, Hollywood's Roosevelt Hotel, its neon-red sign an icon of the silver screen.

Places her parents had never seen.

MacKenzie eased off her other shoe and brought her foot up to rub the stress from her cramped toes. "Could we stop by Patrick's Roadhouse, maybe pick up a banana cream pie?"

Tony flashed her a smile again in the mirror, and it was the first genuine thing she'd seen all day.

She closed her eyes, forcing herself not to see Nils with Isobel.

"A whole pie, or just a piece, ma'am?" Tony said, pulling up to the Roadhouse. The place teemed with people, some eating out on the patio, and hers wasn't the only limo in the parking lot.

"Just a piece would be perfect."

It wasn't her mama's banana puddin', but then again, the Roadhouse didn't have the secret ingredient, the taste of love, in stove-top-cooked cream, stirred with a wooden spoon, her mama's hand cradling hers.

Oh brother, she was turning into a country song in the middle of a parking lot. Next thing, she'd dissolve into a *y'all* while she was *fixin'* to dive into her *paeh.*

Tony returned with the pie in a Styrofoam container, and she gave barely a second thought to the four-digit Chanel creation before she tucked the napkin into her neckline and dove in. She did manage to refrain from licking the container. She used her finger instead, just for Mama.

They pulled into her winding, cypress tree bordered drive and stopped at her front portico.

The starlight sparkled through the hovering palms as she stepped out onto her terra-cotta-tiled porch and handed Tony the bag with her fork and empty container. Then she scooped up her shoes, dangling them from her fingers, and tiptoed up the walk.

She opened the front door—Tony must have unlocked it remotely—and dropped her shoes onto a padded rattan bench, flicked on a light. "Marissa?"

No response from her housekeeper. Tony walked in behind her, carrying her purse. "Everything okay, Miss Grace?"

She glanced at him, and something about the way he looked past her, to her open living room, made her pulse turn to slurry. "What is it?"

The light pressed away the shadows of the main room, glaring on the white leather sofa, the mahogany side tables, a shiny bookcase filled with souvenirs from Paris, Monaco, South Africa. Overhead, the fan stirred the smells of the freshly potted gardenias, brought in for her arrival home yesterday. Beyond that, the dark bank of windows led to the pool area, but her gaze fixed on the center of the room, at the white, misshapen mass atop the glass coffee table.

"Did you have that shipped? Because it wasn't in your

luggage." Tony touched her arm ever so briefly, then moved past her, toward the object.

"No . . . I've never—"

He reached it and yanked the cover off.

MacKenzie fought the swirl of delight. Nils hadn't forgotten. No, he'd remembered their joke, her first red carpet appearance, when she'd nearly ended up on her face in front of Meryl Streep. MacKenzie the Elephant.

So, he'd given her an elephant for the Oscars every year since.

A bronze elephant on her coffee table. A china elephant in her kitchen. An impressionist print of an elephant over her fireplace.

And this year, a nearly life-sized stuffed baby elephant, wrapped in a magnificent yellow bow.

Oh, Nils.

So, maybe she'd forgive him for not mentioning her tonight in his litany of thank-yous. He clearly remembered what they'd had together, knew what she'd meant to him. "I can't believe—"

But Tony had finished reading the card, and when he turned, his expression stopped her cold. Chilled her to the bone.

No—Not again—

And that's when she heard the ticking.

Tony had slapped his arm around her waist and was already tackling her to the floor when the bomb exploded.

Luke took one look at his father and wished he'd never come down from the mountain.

"Pastor Alexander is having a good day today," said nursing assistant Missy Guinn as she wheeled William Alexander III into the community room. She set the brakes on his wheelchair, adjusted his soiled bib, and patted his shoulder before leaving him to celebrate his seventy-second birthday with a family he only sometimes recognized.

Really? A *good* day? Luke ran his gaze over his father, his chest tightening as he took in the glazed eyes, the soggy dress shirt, the big, arthritic hands positioned on the tray attached to his chair, the way he listed to one side. Because this didn't look like a good day for a man who once stood six two and practically knew the Bible by heart.

Luke tightened his hold on his lukewarm, stomach-rot coffee, hoping to shore up his courage. He'd promised Ruthann he'd stay. At least until the cake. Especially since this was the old man's first birthday without their mother.

"Hey, Daddy." Ruthann pressed a kiss to her father's tissue-paper cheek and wiped the corner of his mouth. "Happy Birthday."

She stepped away, and it seemed to Luke that maybe the old man followed her with his eyes. Maybe that was just wishful thinking.

He knew he should greet his father, but he couldn't move from his post by the wide picture windows overlooking the grounds—a few barren picnic tables, the grass yellow and crunchy under the crisp Tennessee air, the oaks still, their bare arms reaching up to the murky gray sky as if in supplication for spring.

"Uncle Luke, look at me!"

Luke looked down just in time to see his six-year-old nephew, Trevor, sail by in an unoccupied wheelchair. He caught the back handle, arresting the forward motion.

"Whoa there, Andretti. Whose wheels did you boost?"

Trevor grinned, revealing a gap where his two front teeth

should be. "I found it over there." He pointed to a gathering of the elderly watching *Jeopardy*. Or, appearing to watch *Jeopardy*. Luke pinpointed the victim of the lost wheels as the tiny woman snoozing in the recliner.

"Return the hotrod, pal." Luke gave him a slight push. "And keep it under the speed limit."

"Always a cop, even when you're out of the park," Ruthann said, shooting a glance at her son. Clearly she didn't see the problem with him tooling around the nursing home. Then again, they spent a lot more time here than Luke. "I'm not a cop, Ruth. I'm a park ranger. There's a difference." Although, admittedly, up on the mountain, in the backwoods of the Appalachian Trail, not much of one. At least not this weekend.

"Then what's with the shiner?"

Luke's mind flicked back to the so-called hunters he'd happened upon, the ones on the ATVs, who'd managed to double-team him before getting away. He'd put a warrant out on them for poaching.

"I had a run-in with a Siberian tiger."

Ruthann's jaw tightened. "Funny." She pushed their father to the table where she'd already lit the chocolate layer cake, smoke curling from the chunky numbered candles—seven and two.

Seventy-two short years. Most men at this age should be on the golf course, touring Scotland, or fishing with their grandson. Especially a decorated Vietnam vet, a faithful husband of thirty-five years, and long-time pastor of the Normandy Ridge Community Church.

Alzheimer's was a cruel thief.

"Come over here and blow out these candles with us." Ruthann shot him an undisguised, *Help make this good for Daddy* expression.

Hey, *he'd* wanted to do this outside, maybe bundle up his

9

father, wheel him out to a picnic table, let him smell anything other than the trapped, piped-in air that probably sucked the life out of him with each breath.

Luke's judgment wasn't fair, and he knew it. The home had kind aides, and he'd never seen his father neglected. Yet, with everything inside him, he wished his stomach didn't turn to knots, his palms slick with cold sweat, his legs quiver with an almost Pavlovian urge to bolt every time he saw him fading away in his wheelchair.

Like now. Luke pried himself away from the windowsill and forced his body to the table in obedience to his sister's request.

He managed to set down his coffee without spilling it and leaned over to his father. "Happy birthday."

Ruthann was straightening his father's bib, trying to prop him upright. "For a guy who's not a cop, you certainly get in enough scrapes. I'm just saying that it doesn't look like the Appalachian Trail is any safer than the jungles of Mexico."

Yes, probably it seemed the same to her—a woman who had her life tucked neatly together with her beloved son, her own business, her accountant husband, her three-bedroom house with the front porch attired in rocking chairs, as if already preparing for their retirement years.

"Let's blow out the candles, Pop." He crouched beside his father and, to his surprise, when he looked over at him, he saw someone there. Someone who knew him, who had nursed him through his nightmares when he'd arrived home six years ago, broken and jumping at his own shadow.

Most of all, Luke saw the soldier who understood the difference between Mexican drug lords and a couple of illegal hunters on the top of Roan Mountain.

And then, just as Ruthann dove in and blew out the melting candles for all of them, his father moved his hand off his tray.

Touched him.

Luke stared at the hand, once strong and firm, now warm and soft on his. His breath hiccupped, and suddenly he could only hear the whirring inside. Faster, louder, drowning him, filling his throat—he couldn't breathe—

"I think I'm just going to get some more coffee," he said, jerking his hand away, standing. Somehow he managed to sound normal. As if his world hadn't blown apart, right then, into a thousand bloody pieces.

Again.

His sister caught him on the way to the door.

"Stick around, Luke." He looked down at her, and the gentle look on her face stopped him from yanking his arm from her hand. "It'll be okay."

No, it wouldn't. Because regret had teeth, and when he wasn't looking it could gnaw right through him, tear him apart piece by piece. One touch, one memory at a time.

He stepped away from her, probably harder than he should have, and started for the hallway, his breaths coming fast. Too fast. He just needed to make it outside. Get . . . some . . . air—

Antiseptic hit his nose, burning his eyes. Striding down the hall, he kicked a cart of half-eaten food, turned, and caught a bowl of cold chicken noodle soup as it overturned on his hands. It splashed, sticky between his fingers, down the front of his pants.

Setting the bowl back on the cart, he grabbed a napkin, whirled, and headed for the door, his jaw on fire, his chest about . . . to . . . explode—

He slammed through the doors, gulping the cold air, one breath lapping another. Bending over, he gripped his knees, closed his eyes.

And for a long second, he could taste the past—the tinny acid of his own fear, his body, sweaty and rank, the grimy feel of starvation in his teeth. The surreal shriek of his own screams.

"Luke?"

He jumped at her voice, whirled to face her, his fists tight. Ruthann recoiled fast. "It's just me."

Luke clenched his jaw, breathed out hard, forcibly opened his hands. Just his kid sister. Not a couple of thugs dragging him out for a beating.

Ruthann held out a wad of napkins, her gaze flicking to the dribble of noodles down his jeans.

He took them from her without a word, but instead of wiping himself off, he turned back and listened to the snarling Watauga River, just past the grove of trees. The breeze raised gooseflesh on his bare arms, but he drew it into his lungs, glad for its brain-clearing bite.

"Why didn't I come home earlier?"

His voice was so soft, he wasn't even sure he'd spoken—it could have been more of a moan inside. But he had, because Ruthann stepped up beside him, her arms crossed over her chest. "Because you needed to be away."

"I needed to be *here*."

"You needed to get well. To get your life together. And start over. We all understood that. Especially Dad. He didn't want you to know—"

"You should have told me how bad he was getting." He tried to keep the edge out of his tone, but it hit her anyway, and she flinched.

"I did. You didn't answer my e-mails. Besides, it came on so fast, no one could have predicted how quickly he'd go downhill. It's nobody's fault, Luke. You were who you were, and you can't go back."

And that was the problem, wasn't it? He couldn't ever go back, fix it, make it right. Not for his father, not for himself . . .

Luke closed his eyes; tears pooled under them. The wind dried them to an icy glacier.

"I wish . . ."

"You'd been here? Of course you do. But you were here for the good parts."

He couldn't look at her. She said that a lot—a coping mechanism he supposed, something she gleaned from her support groups. Of course, it made sense. Yes, he'd grown up happy, with parents who loved him. Believed in him.

Even when he hadn't believed in himself.

But his wishes went further back than just six years ago, when he was leaving town in a cloud of smoke. And that was the problem . . . his father was forgetting the wrong things, hanging onto the ones Luke wished time might erase from the old man's addled mind.

"Come inside, Luke. Have some cake."

"Miss Ruthann?" Missy Guinn stuck her head out of the doorway behind them. "Have you seen Trevor?"

"He's not inside?"

"No ma'am. I came back to fetch your father, and one of the aides said she saw him pushing a wheelchair down the hall."

"I told him to put that back—"

Luke held the door open.

Ruthann pushed past Missy. "Why didn't she stop him?"

"She was busy with a patient—"

Ruthann had already taken off down the hall in a jog. "Trevor!"

For crying out loud, the kid was probably pilfering someone's candy supply. Luke hotfooted it down the hall, peering into rooms, wincing now and again at the inhabitants. Please God, he never wanted to be that helpless again.

His sister's voice echoed down the halls. Perfect. Maybe

they could make the newspaper. *The Normandy Voice* was always looking for juicy stories.

Especially if they involved Luke Alexander.

He passed by the side double doors leading out to the parking lot and, out of his periphery, he glimpsed a gray blur. Oh no—

Turning, he sprinted to the door, flung it open.

Sure enough, Trevor-the-Terror Andretti was making for the parking lot on his stolen wheels.

"Trevor!"

The kid paid him no mind, wheeling fast as he sailed off the handicap access into the lot. He shot past the few cars at the curb and was out onto the smooth pavement, wheeling along with abandon.

"Whee!"

Luke broke into a run. "Trevor!"

Because it wasn't enough that Trevor was joyriding with the property of the Normandy Ridge Residence Center. He was heading straight for disaster—the inclined drive that led to the highway.

"Trevor, stop—"

But as Trevor put out his hand to stop the chair, it ripped at his arm, and he let out a howl. And of course, now he'd lost control of the wheels, set on a careening trajectory straight into death.

"Trevor, jump!"

A scream behind him—Ruthann had found them.

Luke peeled out into a full run, his heart already ten lengths ahead of him as Trevor turned, holding onto the back of the chair, his big eyes now full of terror. "Help, Uncle Luke!"

Luke lunged for the chair, managed to bang it.

It shot out of his reach.

Brakes squealed, horns, the sound of metal crunching—

Just as the wheelchair hit the barrier between pavement and asphalt, Luke hooked Trevor around the chest and dove.

Skin peeled from his arms, embedding gravel as he skidded into the ditch along the highway, grinding mud into his pores, his hair, his back. He clutched Trevor to his chest.

Ten feet away, two cars had collided, the wheelchair crumpled beneath the bumper of a third.

Trevor struggled in his arms, but Luke held him tight, staring at the gray, sunless sky. Breathing. Alive.

Alive.

And, at the end of the day, that was probably the most important part, right?

Chapter Two

"LEAVING LA JUST FEELS LIKE RUNNING AWAY TO ME, GREG, and the truth is . . . I never run away from trouble." MacKenzie walked to the railing of the rooftop porch, overlooking Manhattan Beach. Greg didn't exactly have a sandy front yard, but from three stories up on his Mediterranean-style home, she could see the Pacific Ocean surfing up the shore past the last gilded rays of the day into the shadows of twilight. Palm trees and volleyball nets along the shore shivered in the wind, and the sun iced the roofs of the neighboring homes with hues of gold.

"No, *Hayes O'Brien, 006*, never runs away. You, MacKenzie Grace, are allowed to run. To hide, to go far, far away, and lay low while the media forgets."

She glanced at Greg, who hadn't risen from the lounge chair behind her. "If I do that, I'm liable to never return." Her wrist still hurt, despite the brace, and she babied it as she pulled her sweater around her. The night crept through the holes and prickled her skin.

"I'm just so tired of being the top headline where everyone is deciding how I might resurrect my career, or declaring my career's over, or even questioning why I would make an indie film, as if that might be some sort of desperate attempt to show that I can act. Did it ever occur to them that I *wanted* to make this film? Because it's an issue that matters?" She shook her head. "I'm just . . . tired."

Bone tired. The kind of tired that came from running too long without stopping to rest. Or even to figure out where she was headed. "I just feel like everyone else has control of my life but me . . ."

"I know the press hasn't been kind—"

"Not kind?" MacKenzie shot him a look over her shoulder. "They've practically eviscerated me. It's not enough that my home is half-torched and that my driver has second-degree burns from protecting me, but now Nils has me practically framing him for the attack!"

"I told you not to talk to the press. You were upset, and no one handles their words well when they're upset." Greg's tone was so quiet, she turned just to make sure she'd heard him correctly.

"Are you blaming me for the media's feeding frenzy?"

"I'm just saying that maybe you shouldn't have given a statement right afterward. Especially one that implicated your ex-husband."

"I did *not* implicate him. I said that every year Nils sent me a gift—and that someone figured that out and used it to get into my house."

"You clearly made it sound like Nils was out to get you. You can't expect his camp to sit on that without responding. And the *Star's* headline certainly didn't help."

MacKenzie cringed. *MacKenzie Grace Suspects Ex-husband, Academy Award Winner, in Attack.*

Yes, that was an unfortunate piece of newsprint.

"Okay, I can admit that I should have just ignored the flashbulbs and mics—but frankly, I'd had it with being the

17

victim. It was time to show I wasn't beat, that I wasn't going to let Hollywood or my ex-husband or some crazy stalker take me down. I just wanted to fight back a little . . . like Hayes."

"Maybe a little less Hayes would've been good. Especially since *Hayes* doesn't have an ex-husband to indict."

"I didn't blame Nils!"

"I know that, but next time you feel the need to fight back, wait for me. I *was* on my way—"

"You were at the *Vanity Fair* party, talking to Posh Beckam, if I recall. I was surprised you even bothered to show up."

"That's not fair, Kenzie. You're my girl. I don't care if I was having a rousing chat with Steven Spielberg—you needed me. And I'm here for you."

Yes, he had been there for her—from the very minute he showed up at the hospital. He'd arranged transportation and security, and a hotel to stay in, and finally a room in his own digs just because she couldn't stop shaking.

"This is why I think you should go away. I'm telling you, Kenzie, it's not cowardice to leave and hide out somewhere. Heal a little bit. You can't exactly throw yourself into another role with a broken wrist."

"Cracked. And I'll be as good as new in no time." Well, okay. She might never be as good as new. A week later, she still needed a sedative to sleep, still heard Tony's moans, still smelled the acrid nose-curling smoke of the elephant and all her mementos burning. Most of all, she still tasted her own fear welling in her mouth as she helped Tony from the house.

"I just want them to find Leon, put him back behind bars." She couldn't believe that her most famous stalker, crazy Leon Hicks, had found her again.

Three restraining orders and finally a stint in prison— wouldn't the guy give up? She returned to the table, picked up the cup of chamomile tea Greg's housekeeper had prepared for her, and sat on the lounge chair next to Greg.

"LA police picked him up yesterday. Unfortunately, he's lawyered up, but they're still holding him while they check out his alibi."

Well, at least she wouldn't have any more exploding elephants on her doorstep. MacKenzie took a sip of her tea. Her cup rattled as she set it back onto the saucer. She ran her thumb down the handle. "Poor Marissa. She didn't know the elephant wasn't a gift—she thought it was from Nils."

As did the entire country, thanks to MacKenzie's babbling.

She just wanted to grab those hours back, not only the ones outside the hospital, when she accompanied Tony into the ER, but going back further, before the elephant, before even Nils, maybe all the way back to the day she'd packed up her Ford Escort and headed to Duke University, riding high on her academic scholarships. Maybe a look backward, to the world she'd left—her mama pressing a paper bag lunch into her grip, and her daddy, hands thick with grease, standing in the doorway of the barn, pride beaming from his eyes as she drove away from the mountain, would help her remember who she should be today.

Whether she should run and hide, like Greg wanted, or stand her ground.

"Listen, we both know the press is having a heyday with your run of bad luck."

"It's hardly bad luck to have someone try and kill you."

Greg held up his hand. "Agreed. But negative press of this kind isn't going to help you raise funds to promote your film. Next time check with me when you want to play producer on an indie film."

"Don't hold back, tell me how you feel—"

"I'd like you to let me handle your career, please. Call me

crazy, but that's what you hired me for. Now, the press will only predict that the film will flop, and you'll be getting negative reviews before it's even screened. Our best bet is to get you attached to a new film, ASAP. In the meantime, lay low for a while. Take a look at those scripts I left on your bureau—"

"Stop! Can you hear yourself? I have a stalker after me, and all you can think about is what bimbo part I'm going to play in my next movie. I told you, I don't want to do those kinds of films anymore. I want to be more than Hayes O'Brien, super spy. I want to be taken seriously and offered roles that will impact people, change lives."

Greg's mouth tightened into a grim line. He wasn't that much older than her—maybe ten years—and, despite his efforts to shave the good-ole-boy persona from his demeanor, he still emitted a certain southern charm that netted him the right tables and handshakes from top-level studio execs. That down-home charisma had been exactly what made her trust him when she'd arrived in LA, her Escort packed to the roof, his name scrawled on a strip of paper.

He wielded his inner gentleman now as he gave her a sad look. "Sweetheart, those kinds of films pay your bills. And, right now, unless I'm mistaken, producing your indie film has sucked every morsel of cash from your account. You need a so-called 'bimbo' part if you hope to fund anymore deep, probing, life-changing movies, or even promote this one." He touched her hand. "Kenzie, I'm on your side. You need money, and I know how to get it for you. You're a good actress, and directors are lining up for you."

She couldn't help the *harrumph* that burped out at his words. "Then tell me why my ex got the Academy Award, and I got 'Best Dressed' by *Hollywood Tonight*."

"Because you *are* beautiful."

"I want to be brilliant."

"I think you're brilliant."

"I pay you to say that."

He smiled. "Whatever you say, honey. I call it like I see it. The fact is, you have plenty of roles you can choose from—just not with the parts you want."

She stared out at the sky, the sun just a rim of simmering light along the black horizon.

"I get it, Kenzie, I do. But give it time. Right now, you're broke, you have no place to live, the cops are trying to nail evidence on your attacker, and it doesn't take a therapist to see how badly you need R & R. I *know* you're roaming my house at night. I also know how much warm milk you're going through—"

"My mama's favorite recipe."

He smiled, and she warmed to it.

"Why can't I just go home? Back to North Carolina?"

"For the very reasons you've never told anyone your real name or the truth about your parents. The press could so easily track you there, and then what?"

MacKenzie closed her eyes. Yes, that would be the last thing her parents needed. A convoy of vehicles tearing up their front yard and the gladiolas along the side of the trailer. She couldn't bear for anything to happen to them. Childhood habits weren't easy to escape.

"Where do you suggest I go?"

Greg finished his drink then balanced the cup on the arm of his chair. "My family has a little cabin, set back in the woods in Tennessee. It's clean and safe, and no one would suspect you're there."

"Aw . . ."

"Listen, you love the Blue Ridge Mountains, and this place is right on the Appalachian Trail. Gorgeous. Fresh air, magnolias, and the song of mourning doves."

"Oh, you make it sound so romantic."

"Could be. You never know. That wouldn't hurt you either."

MacKenzie shot him a thin smile then set her own half-empty cup on the ground. "I don't know. What about my film? What about Tony? And Marissa is scared to death, not to mention jobless, while the house is being repaired."

"I'll check in on Tony and Marissa. And I'll keep an eye on your house. Most of all, you'll be out of the way. Safe. Which will let the cops nail Leon for his crime."

"And it'll keep me off the front pages."

The sun had shuffled below the horizon now. The black, tufted outline of palm trees scrubbed the twilight.

"We'll tell the press you went to a private spa in Turks and Caicos."

"Couldn't I really go there instead?"

"The best part is, I have a cousin who lives out that way. He's former military. I'm going to ask him to check in on you now and again—"

"Greg—"

"Don't give me that tone. You do as I say. Let me straighten out things here, while you read through those scripts and decide which one you want to do."

"What if I don't want to do any of them?"

He sighed. "Then maybe you need to figure out who you are—actress or broke producer. Because at this point, you don't have enough money to do both."

Oh.

"Get away, sweetheart. Back to the life you know. Eat some grits, drink sweet tea, swing on the porch swing, walk Roan Mountain. Relax. Leon Hicks won't track you to the hills of Tennessee. And if he does, I promise, my cousin Luke will know exactly what to do."

Fate knew how to make a man suffer. It wasn't enough that Luke had sacrificed his pride nearly sprinting out of the nursing home. Or that he'd managed to get his mug in the paper, again, after rescuing his rascal-of-a-nephew from traffic. But now, fate wanted him to replay his past, everything he'd spent the past six years hiding from.

Couldn't the world just leave him alone?

Luke stood at the window, cupping his lukewarm coffee, listening to the rain pellet the roof of his Park Service office. Outside, the torrent turned the parking lot into an ocean, although it had given his F-150 pickup a decent bath, scouring the red clay and pine needles from the wheel wells. The price of living on a dirt road back in the hills.

Overhead, lightning veined the steel gray sky and a thick mist clutched Roan Mountain. No wonder he hadn't been able to receive cell service, even after he'd emerged from his mountain cabin. Seven messages beeped when his phone came to life—three from his sister, one from an unknown, and three from Greg. Clearly, being a hermit had it advantages. Like, not having people pry into his life. He couldn't believe he'd let Ruthann talk him out of fishing in the Watauga, or even—thanks to the thunderstorm—reading one of the books stacked by his stone fireplace, and into the insane idea of letting some reporter for the *Nashville Parade* interview him about Trevor's near miss.

What was her name? Katie? Kimmy? Karen?

If he didn't feel like he owed his sister a favor after all the hours she logged at the care center—hours he should be helping shoulder—he would have told the reporter to sniff around elsewhere. But according to Ruthann, a mention in the big-city paper just might stir the tourism trade.

Normandy's annual Memorial Day celebration had drawn less than spectacular crowds over the past two years.

Normandy needed the money.

The vets deserved the recognition.

And he would never turn his back on a chance to support the real heroes in the world. He just hoped that the rehashing of his nephew's rescue wouldn't turn into an account of the rescue six years ago that landed him on the front pages of newspapers and magazines across the nation.

Could it really be called a rescue mission if a man got his best friend killed?

It didn't matter. Even this media blurb made him ever so grateful that he lived off the grid, without telephone or electricity. Thanks, he liked the Stone Age. Despite Kathy's, or Kacey's or whatever-her-name-was's agenda, he had full intentions of turning the interview on its end, focusing it instead on his father, on the medals the old man had won, and finally honor him for his courage.

It was the least he could do after all his father had done for him.

And, he didn't know how much longer he could spin the lies behind Captain Luke Alexander without having the truth break free. Nothing like been treed.

He watched a forest service truck pull up, splashing through the puddles. Cooper Hale emerged, pulling up the green hood of his slicker as he ran inside.

The office shook as he shut the door behind him. The guy had the grace of a black bear, and the girth to match it.

"Like to drown me out there," he said, shooting a glance at Luke, then around at the bare, wood-paneled office, the handful of desks, the reception area. "What're you doing here? I thought you had the weekend off."

"I'm meeting someone." Luke took a sip of coffee, made a face. "This stuff is awful."

"Did you make a new pot?" Cooper shrugged out of his jacket, hung it up, and ran a hand through his recently mowed black hair. He walked over to the pot, the coffee more sludge than liquid, picked it up, and made a face.

"No. I microwaved it."

"Then it's yesterday's dregs." Coop poured it out. "I've been checking the service roads. So far, the Doe River hasn't washed out any roads, but it's getting nasty out there."

Luke walked over to the sink, threw out his coffee. For once he wouldn't mind a washed-out road. He couldn't take another round of scrutiny. Not when it meant seeing Darrin's bloodied, tortured body in his nightmares again. Or that of little Luis.

"Hey, is that your coat buzzing?" Cooper asked as he pulled out a coffee filter.

Luke glanced at his own still soggy rain slicker hanging on the hook next to Cooper's. "Probably. I don't know why I have a cell phone. People can find you anywhere."

Cooper gave a harsh laugh. "Oh yeah, I know your celebrity status is a real pain. It's so hard to have women writing to you from around the nation, offering their hand in marriage, and *whatnot*." He raised an eyebrow at Luke and grinned.

Luke gave him a narrowed-eye glare.

Cooper laughed, measuring out the coffee. "It's not like you're actually participating in the twenty-first century, Daniel Boone. Do you even know how to answer it?" He gestured toward the still buzzing phone.

Luke ignored it. "Funny. It's probably Greg. He's left me three voice mails—which I've ignored by the way—and he's called me twice more without leaving a message."

"Your cousin Greg? Old Budweiser? I still remember when he played middle linebacker. He hit like a bulldozer. How's he doing?"

"He's some hotshot in Hollywood. I don't know how a good ole boy like Greg hooked up with the movie star industry, but apparently, he still likes to get me into trouble. He's probably calling about our annual fishing trip."

"Didn't he bring out a couple of sissy actors last time?"

"Yep. Like to get us all killed. They made a campfire, nearly set the Cherokee forest ablaze."

Cooper reloaded the coffee and filter into the machine. "Didn't they lie about hanging the bear bag?"

Luke reached into the pocket of his jacket, hit the ignore button for the call to go to voice mail. "Hm mmm. I caught a black bear rooting through our lunch. We finally had to hike out a day early because one of the geniuses snagged a hook on his ear."

"Ouch."

"Oh, yeah. He was screaming about his pretty face. Greg was trying to keep him calm. I wanted to dump them both into the river."

Luke stared back out the window at the deluge of rain. "I don't think I'll be answering Greg's messages, thanks."

Cooper scanned the bulletin board for the day's weather reports and other USDA updates. "So who are you waiting for?"

"Some reporter outta Nashville—I can't remember her name. Evidently, she couldn't find me, so she called my sister. Caught my name in the article in the *Voice*."

"Captain Luke Alexander to the rescue, saving cats and small children." Cooper grinned at him as the coffeemaker gurgled.

"Funny. What was I supposed to do? Let the kid get flattened by a semi?"

"Of course not. I'm just saying that even a redneck like me can figure out this reporter isn't just interested in an interview, if you know what I mean." He glanced at Luke.

"Another reason to stop hiding in the woods, pal. Your non-existent social life."

Luke shot him a *please, don't*, but Cooper clearly still possessed the ability to out blitz him, honed during their high school football days.

"Last time I saw you at a social event was last year's First Baptist annual Sunday school picnic. With . . . hey, how about that—your *sister*."

"Back off, Coop. I don't need any help meeting women."

"*Women*? How about one woman?"

Luke sat down at his desk, opened his computer, and started a game of Spider Solitaire.

After a moment, Cooper picked up on his silence and sat down at his own computer. "I'm just saying, it wouldn't hurt you to engage in a little female companionship." He chased his words with a wink.

Luke shook his head. "Thanks, but I've known near 'bout every girl in the county since birth, and frankly, that's too much information for all of us. If I ever meet anyone, it would have to be someone who didn't know me. A fresh start."

"Good luck with that, pal, because last time I checked, there isn't a woman this side of the Mississippi who hasn't heard of the brave Captain Luke Alexander."

Yeah, that was the problem, wasn't it? Luke moved a black eight onto a nine of hearts. Or, rather, everyone *thought* they knew him.

No, they knew what the army told them. He freed an ace and moved it into an open position.

The front door opened, the cold huff of rain scattered papers from the reception desk.

Drenched to the bone, in her sodden white—was that leather?—jacket, wearing a pair of light-blue suede boots, and designer jeans, a too-skinny woman stood in the

27

doorway, an expression of what looked like annoyance on her face. Water dripped from the ends of her golden blonde hair, and mascara ran down sculpted cheeks from flashing blue eyes. "Okay, I'm here!"

Wearily, Luke closed out his game. Pushed up from his seat. "I'm so sorry, I can't remember your name . . ."

She plunked a rather large, shiny red purse/suitcase onto the reception desk. He noticed an arm brace just peeking out of her jacket sleeve. She favored it just a bit, holding it close to her body. "Really? Oh . . . I thought you were expecting me."

"Of course I am. I'm glad you made it."

"Oh, me too." She stripped off her coat, worked it over her arm brace, and handed it to him. He barely caught it before it slipped to the floor. "You can call me Kenzie."

Under the jacket, she wore a low-cut teal sleeveless blouse, ruffles running up around her neck. A triple strand of what must be costume jewelry held an array of faux sapphires. Someone had come overdressed to the party, despite the conspicuous arm brace, especially in comparison to his faded jeans and flannel shirt. Did she think this was New York?

Maybe he should point out where they were on a map, sandwiched between Virginia and North Carolina, in the far eastern tip of Tennessee, an inch west of the Atlantic seaboard, smack dab in Smoky Mountain territory. Land of bluegrass and honkytonk, not gems and fancy leather.

"Is it always like this?" She tipped her head back, ran her hands through her hair, then tilted her head to the side, squeezing out the moisture onto the floor.

Luke watched it puddle at her feet, still holding her fancy coat.

"Oh, I can't believe I'm out in public like this." She

shivered, head to toe. "And this place isn't exactly easy to find. My driver was lost for an hour."

Her driver?

Still, Luke hung up her coat on a hook.

"Oh, can you find a hanger? I hate having poke marks in my jacket collar. And it wrecks the leather."

Cooper rose from his desk. "I'll get one." He seemed to be hiding a smirk.

"Would you like a cup of coffee?" Luke moved over to the machine, pulled down a mug from the cupboard. Checked it for residue.

"Oh, yes. I'll take a venti sugar-free vanilla latte with lite whip and an extra shot of vanilla. And oh, non-fat, please." She rubbed her hands on her bare arms, now pebbled with gooseflesh. "And one of those butterscotch scones would be epic."

Luke stared into the mug. "Um . . . I think we have some leftover blueberry cobbler? But I'm afraid we're reduced to just plain old Folgers."

"Oh." She lifted a shoulder. "I guess that'll do. Thanks."

He handed her the full mug, and she wrapped her fingers around it. "Oh, warm. I'm frozen to the bone."

Luke watched her blow on her coffee. "So where do you want to do this?"

She looked up, raised an eyebrow. "I . . . I thought you would know."

Oh. Well, "How long do you think it'll take?"

She took a sip, made a face. Clearly the fresh batch wasn't an improvement. "I guess I was thinking . . . maybe a month? I don't know. Depends on how I feel."

How she . . . "A whole *month?*"

She nodded, wandering to the bulletin board, reading the weather reports and other notices. "I mean, probably I'll get

29

bored by then. You know, I have a pretty full plate right now."

"Bored?" He set the coffee cup down without filling it. "I would hate for you to get *bored*." He didn't really expect a cheering section, but he had banged himself up pretty good, and he'd rate it a ten for a high-action sequence. He glanced at the arm brace. Apparently she led a much more exciting life than her appearance let on.

"Me too. Although frankly, after the excitement of the past couple weeks, I'm ready for a little ho-hum."

"Well, we wouldn't want anything *too* exciting would we?" Luke shook his head, moved toward the conference room, hoping Miss Low Expectations would follow. Not that he exactly wanted her expectations higher . . . more expectations would mean more digging. And that would only dredge up pain and memories, regret and more questions.

Yes, ho-hum would be just perfect.

Kenzie followed him, but instead of sitting in a chair, she perched on the oval conference table. Her purse, she'd left in the other room.

She continued to clutch her coffee like a security blanket. She did look cold. The woman needed to look out her window before she got dressed for the day.

"So, what's your first question?" Luke sat, folded his arms over his flannel shirt, stretching out his legs.

Kenzie looked at him. "I just want to make sure this isn't going to be too invasive. I mean, I don't need people following me, taking pictures, intruding into my life. You think you can handle that?"

For crying out loud, it wasn't like she was Woodward *or* Bernstein. She certainly wouldn't find fame from interviewing a guy who'd rescued a kid from a runaway wheelchair. Even if she dug deeper, his history with prescription drugs certainly wouldn't make *Nightline.* Or maybe she'd gloss over that part and find the truth that really might make her famous. He kept his voice nonplussed. "Oh, I think so. I don't think anyone is even going to care."

She frowned. Opened her mouth, closed it. Then, "Well, I don't think that's a very nice thing to say. I mean, I realize that it's not big news anymore, but I do think people will care. I mean, it's not like people won't find out."

"But . . . isn't that why you're here? So that people will . . . find out?"

Her mouth opened in a sort of horror, as if he'd told her that she looked like a drowned rat. With freckles. Definitely with freckles.

"I don't know what you were told, but no, I don't want anyone to know." She got up from the table. She appeared like she might be shaking.

"Then what's the point of meeting with me?"

"Because I thought you were trustworthy." She tightened her jaw, as if sucking in a measure of control. Then, crisply, "I'm sorry, this has been a terrible mistake. Clearly, you're not the man people think you are."

Well, that was the first thing out of her mouth that made sense. And told him that perhaps she already had done her digging. Too much, probably. Which now accounted for every nuance of her strange behavior.

She put down her coffee. "And this is terrible coffee."

Was this some sort of trick to rile him into the truth? Did she think that by her not caring, he'd lower his defenses, get rattled, maybe spill out something new? Sorry, but he knew the rules, thanks to the endless military briefing. "Oh, you're going to have to do better than that, honey."

She rolled her eyes, let out what he'd interpret as a huff of disgust. "*You* made this horrible brew." She picked up her coffee and walked back out into the office. Dumped the coffee into the sink. She washed her hands, then looked for a towel. Seeing none she held her hands up to air dry, like one of those women getting a manicure. "Fine. Listen, I don't know what you were thinking, but I'm not thrilled about hanging around with you, either. So let's just go wherever the cabin is, and get it over with."

"What?" He shot a glance at Coop, who watched the entire transaction with a sort of frown. Luke would have expected a smirk, because apparently Coop's suggestion that this so-called reporter didn't have *reporting* on her agenda had merit. And rocked him, more than a little. She didn't look the type to do, well, *anything* to get a story.

And he wasn't—"This was *your* idea! And frankly, I'm a little offended by it. I'm not sure what my sister told you, but I'm not . . . well, I'm not sure what you're insinuating, but whatever it is, I'm . . . not that type of guy."

She took a little breath, like a pained gasp, and looked as if he'd slapped her. Her eyes even rimmed with moisture. "Excuse me?"

"Yes, excuse you. I think you need to leave, Miss . . ."

"Grace," she said, barely over a whisper. "MacKenzie Grace."

Was that her last name? He thought he remembered it being something else—

"Are you kidding me? You're *MacKenzie Grace*?" Cooper stood up, and Luke turned as the big man hurried toward them both, his expression morphing into something akin to adoration.

His voice even grew soft, less growl, more purr. "What are you doing here, in Normandy?" He picked up a dry, insulated coat from one of the hooks and draped it around her shoulders. She pulled it closer to herself and looked over at Luke as if he'd sold the family farm out from under her. Dangerous emotion simmered in her blue eyes, her blonde hair hung in wet, slightly drying coils. Her jaw tightened, as if trying to keep her mouth from opening and letting out some sort of wail.

He experienced a queasy, raw feeling, not unlike the one he'd felt nearly seven years ago, moments before everything exploded, as he watched little Luis approach the camp, a bag of so-called potatoes over his shoulder.

This was going to get ugly, fast.

"Yes, MacKenzie Grace, the *movie star*," Cooper said, in a between-clenched-teeth-while-smiling stage whisper. "Haven't you ever heard of *Hayes O'Brien, 006*?"

Kenzie continued to stare at Luke, something murderous now entering her eyes.

Luke shook his head, slowly. "Oh no . . . You don't happen to know my cousin Greg, do you?"

Her lips tightened to a tiny knot of fury.

His coat pocket began to buzz.

Cooper led MacKenzie back to the conference room. "Hey, Luke, I think I'd get that, if I were you."

Chapter Three

KENZIE'S CALL TO GREG WENT DIRECTLY TO VOICE MAIL. OF course. "Just what did you tell your cousin?" she said under her coiled breath, all the while smiling at the large, dark-haired man who had finally acted with some chivalry, given her a blanket, and made her a cup of tea.

Not that it tasted any better than the coffee offered by Mr. Lewd Suggestion—at least that's what Luke's *I'm not that type of guy* comment felt like.

It had taken her a long, reeling moment for his meaning to sink in, and well, she wasn't that kind of girl either, thank you very much.

What had Greg gotten her into? And, with whom? She pressed *End* on her phone and snuck a look at him. Luke Alexander. She remembered his name now—thanks to Greg's text.

Park ranger. Local Untamed Wildlife seemed a better description. Who, perchance, needed more monitoring that she did, because her so-called protector appeared a little on the unhinged side, the way he paced in tiny circles, his ear pressed to his cell phone, glancing at her like she might be a wounded deer who wandered in under his watch.

Not that he didn't look capable of taking care of a wounded deer. Or elk. Or black bear. Easily over six feet, he had the lean, broad-shouldered appearance of many of her leading men—with the exception that his toning probably came from good old-fashioned hard work as opposed to the gym and occasional body-enhancement surgery now popular in her neighborhood.

He wore his dark blond hair long, a little unruly, a renegade accent to the solemn set to his clean-shaven jaw as he turned away from her, cutting his voice low, nearly growling into his phone.

She certainly wouldn't want to be the person on the other end of the line.

"So, what brings you to Normandy, Miss Grace?" Cooper, or "Coop," as she had been instructed to call him, asked.

MacKenzie glanced again at Luke, a cosmically unfortunate piece of timing given the fact he'd chosen that moment to hang up, turn, and stare at her as if she might be a mess of roadkill he had to clean up.

Nice. Her thumb hovered over Greg's speed dial. "I'm here on . . . vacation," she said. She broke away from Luke's decidedly lethal gaze and stirred the tea, then spooned out the bag, pressing it against the side of the cup.

"Vacation? In Normandy?" Coop, who reminded her a little of a much younger Jim Belushi, pulled out a chair and sat down opposite her, as if ready to hear her life story. "No one ever comes to Normandy to vacate." He bit off the end of his word with a smile and a chuckle. "At least not big movie stars."

She held up her hand. "Actually, I'd like to keep my presence here on the down-low. That's why I . . . picked Normandy." She smiled at him, a conspiratorial look she

35

dragged up from 006, and pressed a long, manicured finger to her lips.

"Oh," he said. He mimicked her. "Gotcha."

Luke strolled over to her, every step weighted with a sort of sigh. He leaned against the doorjamb, folding his arms over his chest. Considered her a long moment as she sipped her tea.

"Should I be apologizing for something? Because it seems to me that you were the one with the ugly assumptions," she said.

He ran his hand over his cheek. She couldn't read the emotion in his eyes—half frustration, maybe annoyance?

What did he have to be frustrated about? It wasn't like he would have to camp out on her doorstep. And he wasn't the one who had to pick up his life and run halfway across the country. He didn't have his name and face splashed across every rag in the country: *MacKenzie Grace in Hiding.* She'd wanted to clean out the entire rack when the driver stopped for gas at the local airport. Why hadn't she insisted on renting a car instead of letting Greg arrange an airport limo? Now she was trapped here—or in whatever backwoods location he decided to dump her.

"No, I didn't get Greg's message until now."

Oh. She replayed their unfortunate conversation and didn't know how to unsnarl it. From his death-row expression, looking after her appeared to be the very last thing Luke Alexander wanted to spend the next month doing.

And now she'd gone from being a victim to being a hassle. Perfect.

"I'm sorry to put you in this position, Mr. Alexander—"

"Call me Luke."

"Then, Luke. Maybe I should just call Greg and tell him—"

"No, he briefed me on the situation." Luke's gaze flitted to Coop, back to her. "I'll take you up to the cabin, make sure you're snug as a bug, and keep an eye on you until Greg tracks down some full-time security."

"But I don't want someone babysitting—"

The front door opened, and with it, a peel of thunder. Rain splashed into the room as a yellow-slickered form entered, shaking off a red umbrella. "Is Luke Alexander here?"

Luke leaned up from the door, another heavy sigh escaping.

Kenzie watched as he sulked over to the woman—a petite brunette with eagerness written all over the way she introduced herself—Candy Sloan, with the Nashville Something—and practically lunged for Luke's proffered hand.

Luke offered her a cup of coffee, and then, glancing at the conference room, gestured toward his desk.

MacKenzie could have been dreaming it, but the guy had gone from tightly wound to about to snap.

Interesting.

"Why is she here?" she asked Coop, keeping her voice light. From the way the clerk in the store gawked, and Coop's delayed reaction, Kenzie guessed she looked more drowned rat than superstar MacKenzie Grace. For once being tired, crabby, and disheveled would do her a favor.

"Luke saved his nephew from being pancaked by traffic last week—and he's sort of a local hero, so they wanted to do a story on him. Apparently she's doing a follow-up special interest piece."

A local hero. *He's former military.* Greg's words pinged in her mind as she watched Luke sit down, fold his hands over his chest. He looked at the woman as if he wanted to turn her into a pile of ash.

A smile touched MacKenzie's lips. So, apparently she and Luke had something in common—a hatred of the press. Or at least a vivid wariness.

"If he doesn't want to be interviewed, why is he doing it?"

"His sister asked him to do it. She's head of the Chamber of Commerce in town, and apparently tourism is down. Normandy has a big World War II remembrance every year, and she thinks a nod in a national paper will increase our website hits."

"A national paper?"

"Well, Nashville isn't exactly national, but we get a lot of traffic from the big city. She's doing a piece about everyday heroes—although Luke is anything but *everyday*."

Oh, she could see that.

Candy—really, that was the byline she wanted to use?—set up a tape recorder and began to pepper Luke with questions—although, from the conference room, Kenzie couldn't make out Luke's nearly monotone, one-syllabic answers.

"What did he do?"

"His nephew was making a quick getaway on a boosted wheelchair. Luke tackled him just as it flew into traffic."

"No, I meant in the military."

Coop sat down across from her, having found a package of Lorna Doones. He opened them and set them in front of her.

"He was a special forces soldier, and he and his team went in to rescue this DEA agent a few years ago. Only, he and his friend got taken. He was held hostage for about six weeks—everybody thought he'd died. And then, he escaped. With the DEA agent. He was a hero—except for the fact his buddy died trying to escape. Luke's never got over leaving him behind."

Coop helped himself to a cookie. "It made the news—big

time magazine article, exposing the drug lords of Central America. Luke even appeared on *GMA* and the *Today* show."

"Why did he leave the military?"

"He was injured too, in the escape. Nearly lost his leg. Took years of physical therapy."

Kenzie watched Luke now as Candy leaned in, asked something that made his breath intake. He shook his head.

She raised an eyebrow and then pulled something from a file folder. Asked him another question.

Even from where she was, Kenzie could see his recoil. His eyes flashed, then, with some sort of pain.

Kenzie found herself on her feet, edging out the door, toward Luke.

"I'm not going to talk about that," Luke said, almost a growl.

"Is it true that you've never talked to his widow about what really happened? Because in her book, *Dark Secrets*, she says that you left her husband to die—"

"Is that what this is really about?" Luke had now found his feet. "I'm not doing this. I agreed to talk to you about my nephew's rescue, not face some wild accusations—"

"Is that what you're calling leaving your friend behind to be tortured by drug runners?"

"I told you to leave it alone!" Luke thundered.

"What are you hiding? The public deserves to know the truth!" Candy stood and jabbed the recorder at Luke, clearly unable to see the torment that raked across his face. Unable or maybe, uncaring.

But Kenzie saw it. A raw, bone-deep pain that rocked him back on his heels, and if she wasn't mistaken, slicked sweat across his face. "This interview is over," he said tightly. "Get out."

Get out. How many times had she wanted to say that to some reporter? Or, better yet, say, how would you like to have your life exposed for the world to see? And seeing Luke turn away, stalk toward the back windows, nearly shaking, well, something akin to comradery turned inside her.

Why did the press think they could take a rumor and turn it into a headline? Why did they get to own a person's privacy?

Candy shook her head to Luke's less than polite request, and Kenzie had the sudden urge to shake *her*. But the woman pocketed the recorder with a, "we're far from done, Mr. Alexander."

She turned on her heel and headed toward the door, nearly bowling Kenzie over as she breezed by.

Almost without realizing she was moving, Kenzie followed, hot on Candy's tail. "Excuse me—"

Candy turned, her eyes landing on MacKenzie with some disgust. Despite Kenzie's relief at not looking quite herself, Candy's redneck disdain, not to mention her rather snarky, "What?" stirred her ire.

"You know, maybe you should just leave him alone. What gives you the right to pry into someone's past? He clearly doesn't want to talk about it. How would you like someone to dig around in your backstory, maybe drag up a few skeletons?"

"The public has a right to know what really happened."

"Oh, pu-*leaze*. You're only interested in selling magazines or"—she leaned down close to Candy—"are you intending on selling this article somewhere . . . else?"

Candy had a lousy poker face. "You tell your friend that this thing isn't going to go away. The truth will find him out." She looked over Kenzie's shoulder. "He's not the hero everyone thinks he is. Unless hero is a euphemism for murderer." She banged out the door.

Kenzie watched her go, splashing through the puddles as the rain slicked her coat to her body.

Everything inside Kenzie tremored. She shook her head, turned, ready to launch into a loud dissertation about the evils of unchecked journalism, when her gaze landed on Luke.

He sat propped against the desk, his arms folded across his chest, and the look he wore she wouldn't define as friendly. Then again, she wouldn't exactly peg it as hostile either. Maybe more . . . annoyed. Even, confused.

"What?" she said. Excuse her, but she'd been watching his back. Which, after their rather rocky start, should earn her a few points.

He pushed up from the desk, walked toward her. "You'd make my new job a lot easier if you'd refrain from taking down the local reporters."

"Your new job?"

"As your tour guide-slash-bodyguard?" He raised an annoying eyebrow.

"I would have thought a thank-you might be in order. Besides, you let her walk all over you. You have to handle her. Now she's only going to reload and launch another attack, this time with more ammo."

"Oh, I have no doubt she'll be back." He picked up a baseball cap from a hook then slid on his coat. "Especially since she's right. Let's go."

He left her standing there, as he stomped out to the truck.

Luke didn't know who to strangle first—the blonde sitting beside him in the cab of his truck, or his cousin Greg, at home at his place in LA; neither of whom could mind their own business and leave him alone.

"I was just trying to help," MacKenzie said. "I just hate the fact that they think they can rule the world."

"It really wasn't any of your business, Miss Grace."

"It's Kenzie. And . . . I know." She sighed, looking away. "Reporters just . . . get under my skin. A hazard of the job, I guess."

"A hazard of your job?" Luke glanced at the brace on her wrist. He had to admit, he hadn't the faintest idea who Hayes O'Brien, 006 might be, or why she wore the brace, but judging by Cooper's expression—full out admiration—Hayes O'Brien was clearly *someone*.

Enough of a someone to be the subject of a stalker, according to Greg. *Just keep an eye on her, look out for anyone or anything out of the ordinary. She's mostly spooked, and just needs a place to relax.*

Perfect. And he'd get to play tour guide/bodyguard/innkeeper.

Luke looked away, then back to the road, barely missing a pothole. "Be glad she didn't recognize you. Greg said you're supposed to stay under the radar."

MacKenzie had to brace her hand on the dash, lurching toward him as the truck jolted.

"Sorry."

She glanced at him, her expression soft. "I really am sorry I butted in. And you're right. The last thing I need is some reporter recognizing me. We'd have the national media on our trail in a second. You just looked . . ." She shook her head. "Never mind."

"What? How did I look?"

She pulled in a long breath. "Can we just . . . start over?"

They'd turned off the main highway, and even the winding side road, and now trekked a dirt trail that led to his cabin—or he should say, the Alexander family cabin, as Greg's side of the family technically owned it also. But most of his clan had moved on—farther west, others down to Georgia. He'd thought the place free and clear for his use . . .

"Not until you answer my question. How did I look?"

"Luke, I'm around actors way too much. I probably see things that aren't there. And really, it isn't any of my business, like you—"

"Stop stalling, Miss Grace." Luke glanced at her, his chest tightening. He'd spent years grooming his expression to hide his past. How could she—

"Tortured. You looked tortured. There, happy?"

No, not especially.

"The reporter mentioned a name, and you got a look on your face that made me think she probed too deep, maybe touched a dark place."

How Luke hated that, in an instant, this stranger had glimpsed a piece of the darkness he'd tried so hard to hide. Or perhaps run from. Or both, depending on the day.

He'd simply frozen when Candy mentioned Darrin's wife, Patsy Gerard. And the fact she'd written a book about Darrin, and the raid in Mexico. Or, at least about what she believed happened. What had she called it? Something about dark secrets? Yeah, that was an understatement.

"Why did that reporter say that?"

Luke cut his eyes her direction. "Say what?"

"Earlier, back at the office, about not being a hero? She said you were a . . . murderer."

The rain bulleted the windshield, and he turned the wipers up higher. "I think now is a good time to start over."

So, clearly he wanted to change the topic. She considered him for a moment. "Okay. Sorry. It's the actress in me. I see something in a person, and I like to know where it came from. It's a part of getting inside someone's skin to understand them, and perhaps, eventually, emulate that emotion for the screen."

She couldn't emulate the torture of watching a child die in front of her eyes. Or the desperation of your best friend's hot blood pouring through your fingers.

Still, she did seem to be able to read someone at a glance, while he had the sensitivity of a moose. He'd practically called her a tramp. Even as he thought it, one eye closed in a half-wince. "By the way, I can't believe I said . . . well, what I said to you earlier. I'm sorry about that."

She must be trying as hard as he was, because she offered a laugh. "Yeah, I had to admit, it threw me. But I've been called worse . . . recently." Her voice ended with a sigh.

"Oh, really?" He slowed the truck as he came to a narrow bridge. Under it, an offshoot of the Doe River rushed in a white, angry swirl over rocks and downed logs through the woods. Sometimes, after a hard day's work, he'd come down here, find a notch in the rocks, and let the rapids pour over his aching muscles. But after a rain like today, it could sweep him right over, slam his head against a boulder, drown him in three feet of water. "Media?"

"How'd you guess?" She offered him a brothers-in-arms smile. So, maybe they could be friends. Of a sort.

The wooden bridge creaked as he eased over it. Kenzie glanced down, out her window. "Is this thing safe?"

"Yes. I check it every spring. It's just fine."

She had taken her hand off her wrist brace and now it whitened on the door handle.

"Really, we'll be fine. It's sturdy enough."

"Where are we going?"

"My cabin."

"Your . . . *cabin*?" She shot him a look. "Greg told me it was a vacation home."

Uh oh. Greg had called the old log homestead a *vacation* home? Perfect. Yep, it was decided—he'd strangle Greg first.

"I guess you could call it that. It's a two-room cabin with

44

outdoor plumbing and a wood fireplace, useful for hunting and hiding out. Of which, I think you'll be doing the latter."

She glanced at him with wide blue eyes. Pretty blue eyes, he noticed. Yes, they'd make an impression if you saw them on the big screen.

"Did you say outdoor plumbing?"

He grimaced, hating his answer. "Yes. We have a hand pump over the sink, but the facilities are behind the house . . ."

She closed her mouth, and by the angle of her jaw, he guessed that he'd have to stand in line for dibs on Greg.

She shook her head. "I guess it does sound like a good place to hide."

"Greg didn't say much—just that you'd been in some sort of trouble." Actually, he'd used the words *stalker*, and *spooked*. Luke kept his words casual, light. No need to spook her more. A wounded wing and no plumbing—he actually felt a shard of pity for her.

She lifted a shoulder. "Greg thinks someone tried to kill me." Her voice matched his—light, easy, as if hoping not to spook him, either.

Tried to kill— "What? Someone took a shot at you?" Okay, *stalker* might not have been the word he'd have used. Clearly Greg needed an overhaul on his communication skills.

"A bomb. In my living room. We think it's a stalker from the past, but the police aren't sure." She said it without the emotion he expected from an actress. As if she might be, as Greg suggested, very spooked, and trying to hide it.

He'd play along. "That looks like it hurts." He nodded to her brace.

She slid her hand over her arm. "It hurts, but I've done worse. Like the time I jumped out of a moving car and missed the landing pad."

"Jumped out of a moving . . . You're a stunt woman too?"

She laughed. "No, just a young and overzealous actress when I first started. I thought I should do all my own stunts. Not anymore. Now I let the professionals do all the heavy lifting."

"How long have you been in the movie business?"

"About six years. I got a lucky break out of college. Found Greg, and he landed me a bit part in an action-adventure movie. Maybe you saw it? It was called *Lethal Chase*. From there, they cast me as Hayes O'Brien, 006."

"I'm sorry, I haven't heard of it. But it sounds like a James Bond movie."

She gave him a long, almost disbelieving look.

"Sorry, I don't watch movies."

"Oh. Well, she's a . . . takeoff of Bond, only she's American . . . whatever. I've done three of them now."

Silence pulsed between them.

He had to slow the truck to ease around a deep puddle. One wheel dipped in, lurching her toward him again. Low hanging tree branches scraped the top of the cab.

Kenzie righted herself. "Why not?"

"Why not . . . what?"

"Why don't you watch movies?"

"I prefer quiet. Reading. And, the cabin doesn't have electricity."

She closed her eyes as if in pain. Then shook her head. "That's just awesome."

He smiled. "You'll get used to it. I live off the grid, so I still have lights, via the river we passed. And gas lights if I need them. But you learn to go to bed early and get up with the sun."

"Get up with the sun—that's usually when I'm going to bed." But she said it with a tone that suggested she might be stretching the truth. And, underneath that glitz and sparkle—

and especially since she still wore Cooper's raincoat—he suspected that she was a read-a-book-in-bed, get-up-early-and-run kind of girl.

"Mmmhmm," he said. They rolled into a clearing and stopped before the Alexander family cabin. Luke sat in the seat, watching Kenzie out of his periphery as she surveyed her . . . vacation home.

A low-hanging porch with smooth-as-tanned-leather polished wood beams holding up the roof disguised much of the cabin's beauty—the leaded glass windows, the hand-carved door, the river stone fireplace that cut through the center of the cabin for heat, as well as cooking.

"How old is this cabin?"

"About . . . maybe, a few . . . decades."

She slowly turned in her seat. "Guess for me. How many . . . decades?"

"Eight?"

"Nice. It looks like something out of an old western. A real live log cabin."

"Well, it is a real live log cabin. My grandfather cut the trees right here, from the property. In fact, the Alexander family passes down a sort of superstition about Great-Great-Grandpa still lurching about the eighty acres of Cherokee forest, putting tar in the gaps in the logs or fixing the roof, especially on cold nights when the wood moans. It makes for delicious ghost stories for my nephew."

And yes, it might have something to do with the fact that Luke had never gotten around to installing electricity. Or plumbing.

Besides, he had the Air Stream, parked on the other side of the house, if he got desperate.

She sat still, holding her arm, staring at the house. He couldn't read her expression—curiosity? Horror? "Ready?"

Oh no, her gaze appeared stuck on a small building down a thin trail toward the back of the house. "Is that the . . ."

"Biffy. We call it a biffy. Or throne, depending on your mood."

She winced. "Right."

"Ready to face the 'vacation home?'"

"Clearly, Greg's definition of a vacation home and mine need to align more."

He hid a grin. "Stay put. I'll come around and—"

But she'd already hopped out, made a dash for the porch. Ho-kay.

He caught up just as she eased open the door and stepped inside.

Calling it two rooms veered on the side of generous. No one really considered the loft a second room, since it didn't have a door. Or walls. As he peered over her shoulder, he shot a small prayer of gratitude to the army for teaching him how to make his bed and keep his room clean. In front of the fireplace, on one side of the two-sided hearth, an overstuffed denim sofa faced the heat, flanked on either side by homemade hickory furniture. Books stacked beside the chair balanced a cold cup of coffee.

His gaze whisked across the Hudson Bay blanket over his double bed in the corner, the duffel of clean clothing he had yet to fold and put in the trunk at the end of his bed. A bowl of hardened oatmeal remains sat on the sink. He hadn't pumped water yet into the kitchen sink, although now his rain barrel on top of the cabin would surely be filled to overflowing. A red picnic table he'd rescued from a park clean-up crew filled most of the space on the other side of the hearth.

The pungent odor of kerosene mixed with creosote and wood polish, and for the first time he realized how backwoods the place smelled.

"You have a big family," Kenzie said, stopping at the wall near the door, surveying the generations of photos taken. She peered close at a group of teenagers. "Is that Greg?"

"He was a redneck. Don't let him ever forget that."

She tapped the photo then sighed and turned, surveying the place in silence. He watched her face. Yes, she did have freckles, and underneath all that bling, a solidness about her that intrigued him. Did her own stunts, huh?

And, despite his annoyance, okay, it did feel just a smidge good to have someone take up for him. As if she might be on his side.

MacKenzie Grace, movie star. Maybe it was time for him to watch a movie.

We think it's a stalker from the past, but the police aren't sure. Whoever it was, they'd gotten away with it the first time. But Greg had clearly been worried enough to ask Luke to babysit. Which meant this stalker just might find a map and head east, to Tennessee.

And that scenario could only be slightly better than the one flashing through his mind since Candy had dropped the little bomb about Patsy's book.

Luke pushed away the image of reporters stalking him through town . . .

And, right behind that, the image of the people he'd left behind in Mexico, tracking him down through the Cherokee forest right here to this cabin, to finish what they started.

He blew out a long breath, leaned against the doorjamb, folding his arms. Yes, maybe he should be doing the hiding, right along with Kenzie. Because if his whereabouts really got out—not in Tennessee, but into the world at large, she wouldn't be the only one hiding from someone trying to kill her.

Chapter Four

IF THE GOSSIP RAGS COULD SEE HER NOW, THEY'D HAVE A field day.

MacKenzie Grace stars in real-life Deliverance *remake.*

"Make yourself at home," Luke had said as he showed her around the cabin. "There's some venison in the freezer, and a few potatoes left in the bin if you want to eat." He had pulled down a cast-iron skillet from the hanging rack over the work island and slapped it down onto the gas stove.

She stared at it, at the pump in the sink. "Is that where the water comes from?"

He grabbed it, worked a few quick pumps. Water came spurting out. "It's spring water, just about the best stuff in Roan Mountain."

She managed a smile. "Yum."

"Everything here runs on propane," he said, and handed her a box of matches. "Listen, I need to make a quick run up to Nellie's. You'll be all right here for a few, won'tcha?"

It was the Hayes O'Brien inside her that shrugged off his question.

But who was Nellie? His girlfriend? Probably. A man with

Luke's good looks wouldn't go unappreciated for long. She wasn't blind to the way he filled out that ranger uniform, or even the snug fit of his jeans and flannel shirt as he emerged from the Air Stream camper and climbed into the truck. She'd gotten the hint that he was moving out when he grabbed an army duffel bag and hauled it next door. But she ignored the question in her head and managed not to make a pip of alarm when indeed, he fired up his truck and left her in the woods.

Just her and Bambi, some salt, and a container of lard that apparently she was supposed to use to cook with.

No, she didn't particularly prefer a deer steak, thank you so much, Daniel Boone, but apparently man-of-the-woods lived off the land, and so would she until she could find a grocery store and some chicken. Or mahi-mahi.

Or sushi. She could go for a fresh tuna roll with avocado right now.

She'd have to check herself into a spa for an herbal cleanse the second she returned to LA.

If she ever made it back. She might have dropped off the planet for the way the forest closed in over Luke's swatch in the woods. The last lick of sunlight bled through the budding poplar and oaks, and the rain shivered off them, turning the dusk to a sultry amber.

Inside the cabin, the winter clung to the thick wooden walls. Might've been nice if he'd built a fire in that fireplace before he abandoned her.

She looked at the deer meat bleeding onto the counter and shook her head. Fasting never hurt her figure.

Outside, the wind kicked up, moaned through the trees.

Or maybe the moaning came from deep inside, where the memory of a ticking elephant resounded like footsteps in her mind, that moment right before everything went hot and white. She thought she'd escaped it, but it had chased her all

51

the way to Tennessee despite two airplanes, an airport limo from Knoxville, and Greg's best attempts to text her cheery notes about how this was just temporary.

Oh please, let it be temporary.

She walked over to the fireplace and opened the wire screen and with one hand, grabbed a couple logs stacked on the hearth. She'd made a campfire once or twice back in her childhood. Stacking the logs like a teepee, she added a wad of kindling from a basket nearby. It lit quickly and she blew on it a moment to fan the flames. They bit into the dry wood, and she held her hand against the heat for a moment before closing the screen.

See, she could survive Tennessee.

Especially since Luke's cabin did remind her a little of home. The quant, mismatched furniture, the pictures of family hung on the walls. It even sounded like home. The plink of water in the sink, the rattle of the windows in the pane. Of course, her home had thinner walls, metallic ones that shuddered under the breath of a mountain storm. These walls could probably withstand the wrath of Poseidon.

Which meant that probably she was safe here.

The fire spat and coughed out black smoke as it bit into the wood.

By the time Luke returned, the place would be toasty warm.

As for dinner, well . . .

She opened the refrigerator. A bag of apples, a six-pack of Dr Pepper, and a package of beef jerky.

And more Bambi.

She closed the fridge.

Stood in the kitchen.

Heard the thunder of her heartbeat against her ribcage.

Tick.

MacKenzie!

She jerked at the memory of Tony's voice, sharp and violent in her head.

She'd hoped that here, she might throw away the sedatives, but perhaps the silences of the forest only made the attack louder in her memory. With LA around her, she didn't have to stop moving. Didn't have to think.

She'd simply have to figure out how to keep busy here. To push away the quietness of the wilderness of Tennessee. Because if the bombing and the headlines ever stopped stalking her, then the past could easily creep up through the too-familiar smells and sounds, and she'd spend the rest of her time dodging her mistakes.

To survive, she'd have to find something useful to do.

Like figure out why Candy called Luke a murderer.

Or—and probably she should just stay as far as she could from Greg's brooding cousin—maybe she could read over the next Hayes O'Brien script.

She found her bag by the door and took it over to the chair, next to the stack of books, pulling out her collection of scripts. Maybe Luke hadn't been kidding when he said he went to bed with the sun. But by her watch, it was just past eight p.m. Which meant, Pacific time, it was the bewitching hour of five p.m.

Some days she woke up at five p.m.

Like today. Actually, she'd been on an airplane by five a.m., and now, curled up by the fire, her eyes suddenly turned to wax, heavy and drooping.

She got up, pulled the blanket off the bed. The yoga pants and Hard Rock T-shirt she'd changed into clearly wouldn't cut it here in East Tennessee. Neither, probably would the rest of her wardrobe.

If ever she belonged in a Duke sweatshirt and a pair of converse, it was here, among the rednecks.

She settled back on the sofa, picked up the script. Read the first line.

Again.

Maybe just a little nap while she waited for Luke to return. She lay down, pulled the blanket to her chin. For a moment, she returned to the backwater bedroom of her childhood, a narrow, lumpy mattress that punched fists into her back, an army blanket scratching her chin, the moonlight striping the wooden floor like the bars of a prison.

But if that were the case, her mother would be here, pushing her hair back from her face, her doughy outline dim against the Winnie-the-Pooh nightlight. *You're going to change the world someday, ain't ya, Pooh?*

Not yet, Mama.

But maybe, if she could just survive until they tracked down Leon. She closed her eyes.

Oh, how easily her mind drifted back to the smell of smoke, the shouts and flash of pain as Tony tackled her. To the chaos of the police, and Greg arriving at her door. To the ache in her arm. And smoke, so much smoke as her home burned—

"What in tarnation—are you trying to kill us?"

The voice jerked her awake and for a second, she couldn't clear her mind from the tangle of images.

Dark, hazy room, a man in a jean jacket holding a flashlight, his face twisted, the smell, acrid, pinched—she coughed, and her chest knotted.

Then it all returned. The cabin. Luke.

And from the fireplace, black smoke rolled out, angry and lethal.

"You forgot to open the flue!" He held up his shirt, ducked his face into it, then wrenched open the screen, shaking his hand as if he'd burned it. He grabbed a poker, knelt, and reached into the fireplace, up to where the black smoke gathered, billowed out. He pressed the poker into the darkness, and she heard something pop.

Then he turned away, found his feet. "Sheesh, I told you to make yourself at home, not destroy it."

She pressed a pillow to her face, still coughing, her eyes watering.

He dropped his flashlight on the sofa and leaned down, scooping her up without permission and carrying her from the house.

She thought he just might throw her from the porch into the darkness of the yard, but he stopped, his breath sawing, and set her down. "Stay here while I go put it out."

She couldn't protest. Not hunkered over, coughing, her eyes weeping.

Grabbing the front post, she pulled herself to the edge of the steps and sank down, gulping in the cool, damp breath of the night, letting it heal her.

"Next time I ask if you'll be all right, don't say yes." Luke stood above her, a bowl in his hand. Against the darkness, the only light from the high-beams of his truck, he looked more villain than savior, his gaze hard as he dropped the bowl onto an Adirondack chair. "Don't die on me. Greg would have my hide."

"Thanks, I feel . . . much . . ." She let out another cough. "Better."

He looked away for a moment, then shook his head. "Sorry. I arrived back to see smoke drifting past my headlights." He winced. "I might have panicked."

"I didn't know the flue wasn't open. I'm sorry. I didn't mean to catch your house on fire. I was just cold."

She coughed a last time into the pillow. "I'm sorry to be such a pain. I thought . . . I . . ."

And then, shoot, her voice betrayed her and she couldn't

speak. She pressed the pillow to her mouth again. No, she wouldn't cry, wouldn't—

But clearly this had been a terrible mistake. She had no business invading Luke's life. Worse, she'd never survive living in the woods. Not even one night.

What had she been thinking, agreeing to Greg's outrageous plan?

Or even thinking she could be someone who nudged the world, just a little in the right direction. Not to mention that she'd left God and His morals long behind, and she shouldn't think He might show up to help her now.

"Are you crying?"

"No." She blinked the wetness back, but shoot, it just kept coming. "I got some smoke in my eyes."

He stared at her for a long moment then suddenly sat down beside her. "I didn't mean to be gone for so long."

Now that he mentioned it, the cicadas chirruped and stars dotted the sky, pinpricks in the darkness, the storm now blown over. She looked away, managed to stifle the rise of despair inside, and wiped her eyes.

"Did you finish everything with . . . Nellie?"

He turned, frowned, and then, just as the storm that had dissipated, he smiled. And if she wasn't mistaken, he wore humor in his eyes.

He had pretty eyes. Green, with flecks of gold that twinkled in the glow of the headlights.

"Nellie has a post office-slash-grocery store just down the hill. I thought I should pick you up something edible."

"Edible? You mean other than Bambi?"

He gave a laugh, and it released the knot in her chest as he crossed the porch to his truck. He retrieved a paper bag from the front seat. "I didn't really think you'd be frying up venison."

He handed her the bag. "Nellie doesn't stock gourmet, but

I managed to find some yogurt, rice milk, and some bran cereal. I also found you some rabbit food." He leaned over and dug out a head of lettuce. "I'm just checking, but do you eat meat?"

"Of course. Just not the kind with soft brown eyes—"

"That darts in front of cars and eats my plum trees?"

"I just prefer mine in the grocery case, thank you." She looked in the bag and tried out her theory. "Did you and Greg iron out his definition of 'vacation home?'"

He was frowning when she looked up. She raised an eyebrow, smiled. "Nellie's is probably also in cell range, which meant you probably called Greg. Next time you talk to him, ask him what he meant when he said he'd asked you to 'check in on me every now and then.'" She gestured to the Silver Stream camper. "That seems more than stopping by. I had no idea I'd be rousting you from your home."

"It's no problem. I lived in the Silver Stream for over a year. It's home. And apparently Greg said what he needed to in order to push you onto an airplane."

Okay, she couldn't wait. She peeled off the top of the yogurt. "Story of my life. Greg knows exactly what to say to charm me into attending charity events and parties, to lunch with directors who drive me crazy, and even date wannabe actors who end up breaking my heart."

Oh. Now that was probably too much information.

But, thankfully, he didn't bite. Instead, "Greg once talked me into skinny dipping in the Watauga River. Nearly got killed, was swept downstream and picked up by the police in my uh, natural state. It made the papers."

She licked the cover of the yogurt. "He booked me in a fragrance commercial with a lion. I thought I was going to die."

He got up, ducked inside the house where he'd left the

door open. She heard him in the kitchen. "He dared me to ride my dirt bike off a cliff. I broke my collarbone."

"Oh my . . ."

"Missed a month of football practice."

He came back outside, sat next to her, and handed her a spoon.

Sweet. She dug into the yogurt, and it cooled her parched throat. "He knows how to wheel and deal," she said, letting her imagination put Luke into football pads under the bright lights. With wide shoulders and tousled dark blond hair. A good Tennessee boy.

"In this case, I would have to agree with him."

"Yes, I called Greg. And pried. He told me, in great detail, about the elephant bomb, the second degree burns your driver suffered, and your cracked wrist. More than that, he filled me in on the recent news."

His tone brushed a chill through her. "What news?"

"I'm sorry, Kenzie. Apparently *Star Magazine* is running a headline this weekend that suggests you were making the entire thing up as a publicity stunt for your failing career."

Her career wasn't failing. She was just making other film choices.

Oh shoot. Choices that yes, could cost her everything.

"And your ex-husband has decided to sue you for defamation of character."

She stirred the fruit off the bottom, not wincing at the pinch in her side. "Of course he would. It makes for great media and will buy him sympathy right about the time his movie launches." She took a bite of the yogurt. "I made the mistake of spouting off to the media at the hospital. I may have pointed a finger at Nils."

"Are you sure he isn't guilty?"

She heard something more than park ranger in his tone. "Why?"

"It's worse. Your stalker, Leon? He alibied out. He's not the guy."

She licked off the spoon, stirred the yogurt again. "Who do the police think did it?"

"They don't know."

She closed her eyes.

"So yes, I am going to 'check on you now and again,'" Luke said. He glanced at her. "Kenzie, I admit I had no idea what you went through until I talked with Greg. I'm sorry. And I'm going to make sure that no one hurts you, I promise."

His gaze stayed on her, and she couldn't look away. His expression swept the moisture from her mouth, stirred to life something inside she'd nearly forgotten. And not just because his beautiful green eyes had a solidness in them she felt to her soul. No, she couldn't tear her eyes away because, despite his protest to the contrary, she knew, for the first time in longer than she could remember, she had met a hero. A man who would keep his promise.

No matter what it cost him.

Chapter Five

THE REPORTER WAS TRYING TO GET HIM KILLED.

Luke stared at the *Nashville Parade*, his mug on the front, the one taken at the press conference in DC, and wanted to throw the magazine out the cab of his truck, watch the pages flutter to the ditch. Or maybe a semi would scream past, drive a grid across the image of his grizzled face, the one taken by the press after he'd emerged from the Blackhawk. A picture that could still stir up his nightmares if he let it.

So much for keeping the past under wraps. He expected some kind of nod to the past, but the entire front page of newsprint dedicated to the official version of the story? Worse, she didn't stop there but added a review of *Dark Secrets* on the inside front cover.

It made him sound like he'd deliberately left Darrin behind to die.

Maybe people would use the Sunday insert as lining for their bird cages, or dog kennels.

He was thankful Candy hadn't recognized Kenzie. He could only imagine those headlines, and a good bet was that she wouldn't hesitate to make a call to *Hollywood Tonight*.

They made an interesting pair, he and Kenzie, both hiding out in the woods like a couple of hermits. Although he'd have to be blind not to see how each day Kenzie became more restless.

Any day now, he expected her to show up at the local coffee shop, and then the fun would really start.

For now, she seemed grateful enough to park herself at Lucy's Laundry, paging through old editions of *O! Magazine* as she waited for her jeans to dry.

Outside, the beautiful spring day sparkled against the sycamore and black walnut trees, stirring up the fragrance of magnolia, the smells of the Doe River. He should be outside, walking the Appalachian Trail and tracking down those poachers. And he had wilderness EMT certification to update, not to mention a pile of paperwork on his desk in preparation for the upcoming tourist season.

But it was his day to check in with the old man.

He pulled up to the Normandy Ridge Residence Center, parked, and checked in at the reception desk. He felt Missy's eyes on him a little too long as he walked down the hallway, as if he'd been the one to stir up trouble.

Trevor was safely at preschool. Luke had called Ruthann on his routine check-in after dropping off Kenzie. And, he'd also left a voice mail message with Greg, just letting him know that indeed, his megastar was surviving in the woods.

He'd even gotten her to eat a little of his venison spaghetti. Okay, not much. Mostly she spent time reading the library of scripts she'd lugged east with her, and talking to herself.

A lot of talking to herself.

Yes, she might be going stir-crazy.

He knocked at the door just in case his father was awake. Or alert.

The reverend lay in the bed, the television on Animal

Planet, staring vacantly at the ceiling. Luke closed the door behind him.

"Howdy, Pop," he said as he pulled up a chair. He touched his father's veined hands. "It's me, your son Luke."

It helped to identify himself, because just three months ago, his father had stared at him with horror in his eyes, as if terrified.

It dragged up all of Luke's dark memories until he realized that his father didn't recognize him or even remember that night when he'd found Luke high and wielding his special ops skills.

He never stopped thanking God that no one had died that night.

"You're looking good. Missy gave you a nice shave."

Most of the visits of the past months, however, had been for Luke, not his father. A chance to talk to someone who would listen without reproach. Even in life, his father had been that, so it seemed right to return, to let his physical presence help untangle Luke's thoughts.

He had to believe his father was in there, somehow, and would want to know that he was getting better.

In fact, today, he felt . . . well, almost like getting up in the morning wasn't a waste.

"You're not going to believe this, but I have a movie star living with me. A real live actress." He got up, grabbed a hankie from a box on the bedside table, and wiped moisture from his father's mouth.

"She's nice, though. You'd like her. I can hear a hint of a drawl although she's done a good job of turning into a California gal. She's real pretty. Big blue eyes, blonde hair. At first I thought she was a little high-falutin', and you should have seen what she brought to wear. But I fixed her up with some of my old T-shirts. I think she's going to fit right in. She's in a peck of trouble, so she's hiding out." He leaned close to his father's ear. "I promise, there's no hanky-panky going on. I'm staying in the Silver Stream. I told you it would come in handy."

Nothing from his father's eyes. But it made him feel better to say it.

"We got a sort of truce. She doesn't pry into my life; I don't pry into hers."

He went over to the remote and clicked through the channels.

"She's going a bit crazy, I think, but frankly, so am I. I need a fishing trip, take off and do some camping." He settled on a rerun of *Touched by an Angel*. Yeah, wouldn't that be nice. A miracle now and then to convince him that God still cared.

He set down the remote. Sat.

"Patsy has written a book about what happened in Mexico. I haven't read it, but this reporter down in Nashville wrote a review on it. It basically blames me for Darrin's death." He stared at his hands, running a finger along the scar on his palm. "I'm just tired of hiding. Tired of lying. And the worst part is, I'm afraid Lorenzo and his gang haven't forgotten, and they're going to show up here and hurt the people I care about."

"Luke?"

He stilled, and turned at the voice.

What on earth—

"Kenzie, what are you doing here?"

She looked like an east Tennessee girl today, her hair pulled back and up, scant amount of makeup, an old UT T-shirt. Let go of those ugly blue boots, and she'd be a regular co-ed.

"I'm sorry. I called your office to tell you I was finished, and they gave me your sister's number. She said I could find you here."

Oh, Ruthann would have a heyday with this.

She slipped into the room. "You should turn on your cell phone."

Cell phone. "I left it in the truck."

"Right. Well, uh . . . I'm sorry I intruded. I'm going to walk around town a bit. I put the clothes in the back of the truck."

"Walk around town." He glanced at his father. "I don't think—"

He recognized the sudden appearance of Hayes 006 in the way she frowned at him. Yes, he'd done some Internet surfing.

Maybe had stopped by the local Redbox.

He might have even cued up her latest flick on his laptop. Her own stunts, huh?

"I'm fine. Who's going to recognize me?" She slid on a pair of Ray-Bans. Grinned at him.

Maybe . . . "Where are you going?"

"Do you have a coffee shop in this town?"

"Not within walking distance."

Her smile fell, and he felt it in his chest, the sudden dimming of the sun. What was a guy going to do? "I'll drive you."

"Are you sure? You don't look ready to go . . ." She glanced at his father.

"This is my father, Kenzie." He looked at his father, still unresponsive. "The Reverend William Alexander."

She gave Luke a smile, compassion in it. And it could unravel him on the spot, the way she looked at him as if she cared.

He looked away, blinked against the sudden burn in his throat.

"You stay," she said quietly. "I can walk. Or wait."

"I'll be out in a minute," he said, more stiffly than he wanted.

In fact, he longed to take back his tone, maybe explain—

64

except he didn't exactly know what to explain. His regret? His loss?

He breathed out something that felt close to relief when she said, "I'll be outside."

She closed the door.

He sat there, listening to her steps fade, not sure what to do with the tumult in his chest. But he found himself when he turned back to his father. "Don't get any bright ideas, Pop. It's just coffee." Then he leaned down and pressed a kiss to the old man's forehead. "No one got hitched over coffee. Besides, I did mention she was a movie star, right? Fear not."

He found her outside, leaning against his truck, her face to the sky, the sun turning her hair to gold.

"I really am sorry to pull you away," she said as she leaned up from the truck, crossed to the passenger side. "I could walk . . ."

"Get in. I know you need a real coffee."

"Thanks, Luke." She slid onto the cab seat. "My body is craving caffeine. I might have to buy you a coffeemaker."

"And you'd plug it in where?"

She laughed. "Okay, I give up. I've had more sleep in the last five days than I've had in five years. I've read every script twice and even gobbled down that Grisham book you had on the top of your pile. What I wouldn't give for a television. Or a movie." She turned to him. "Please tell me you have a movie theater in town."

"It closed back in '92. But we do have a movie store."

"And I'll watch that on my . . . laptop? While the gerbil runs?" She glanced at him, but her smile didn't look annoyed. "It's okay. Probably does me good to hear my own thoughts for a change."

Probably that was his problem. Too much time hearing his own thoughts. Or listening to them haunt him.

They pulled up to the coffee shop—a local store that

roasted their own beans. "The Coffee Company. Cute." She read the menu board outside for a moment then went inside. He followed her, lured by the smell. He'd forgotten how much he liked fresh ground coffee. Back in his military days, he'd learned to drink it black, like tar. But maybe it was time to upgrade, break free of his regular habits.

He hadn't a clue what to order as she rattled off a prescription for her favorite mix. "Did you have to write that down the first time? A non-fat, sugar-free, what?"

"We call it a 'skinny' in LA."

The girl behind the counter—Luke didn't recognize her—perked up. "You're from LA?"

Kenzie had left her sunglasses on, and now managed to come to her senses. "Naw. I just lived there for a while." She glanced at Luke. Mouthed the word, *sorry.*

But how much trouble, really, could she get in at some tiny coffee place in east Tennessee? He read the menu. "What's good?"

"Try a caramel macchiato. It has vanilla syrup, espresso, and caramel sauce," Kenzie said.

"In coffee?"

"Or an Americano. It's espresso with water added to it. Or a cappuccino. It's got espresso, hot milk, and foam. But have the macchiato. I love them, but my . . . uh, friend Greg won't let me have them. Too brutal on my waistline."

Her size four waistline? Because she already ate like a refugee. "So you want to live vicariously through me?"

"Please." She grinned at him and pushed her glasses up on top of her head.

Oh, she was pretty, her blue eyes shiny. He glanced around the room to see if anyone had recognized her. She wasn't wearing leather, however, and who would expect MacKenzie Grace in a hole-in-the-wall coffee shop in Tennessee.

"I'll take the caramel macchiato," he said to the barista and followed Kenzie to the pick-up counter.

"Some days, all I live on is a skinny vanilla latté for breakfast and a non-fat white chocolate mocha for supper."

"I'm starving you with all this deer meat."

She picked up her drink. "You have no idea." She winked at him before she pulled her glasses back down.

He retrieved his drink and gestured toward a table, but she headed toward the door. "It's so beautiful outside. Let's walk."

He followed her outside without managing to cheer, and they strolled down the sidewalk. He gestured to the T-shirt shop. "This was the first department store in town. Used to be the JC Penney's. And across the street is the Southern, serving the best grits in East Tennessee."

"I know I owe you a debt of gratitude for not serving me a grit while I've been here."

"It's been tough. But certainly you're tired of yogurt, almonds, cottage cheese, and pretzels?"

"I feel like I'm in college again. But no, unless you have a sushi place in town, I'm happy."

"Sushi. Please tell me you're kidding."

She grinned at him, and something sweet and warm stirred inside him. Probably just the macchiato settling in his stomach.

"Up yonder is the monument." He pointed at the obelisk at the end of the street, guarded by two cannons. "It's dedicated to the Union and Confederate veterans from this area. They put it up in 1904."

"This is an old town."

"1799." He guided her toward the Doe River where the covered bridge spanned it. "This is the historic district. There are houses here from the 1700s. And the bridge is over a hundred years old. It was built in 1882."

She stood at a metal rail, watching the foam of the river. "It's gorgeous out here. I'll bet you're swamped during tourist season."

"Not so much. We have a big covered bridge festival every year, and a civil war re-enactment during Memorial Day weekend, but the tourist industry hit a valley with the recession. Hence why my sister wanted me to land that interview."

"Candy. I'd forgotten about her." Kenzie finished off her coffee, turned to face him. He couldn't take his eyes off her freckles. It made her look about nineteen. And cute, like the girl next door.

Uh, she *was* the girl next door. He took a long drink of his coffee, nearly choked.

"Are you okay?'

He wiped his mouth. "Yeah. It's just . . . Candy printed a big article about me in the *Nashville Parade*, but she neglected to mention anything about the Memorial Day event. It's a shame, because we have a lot of veterans here, and the Chamber of Commerce always gives a big Memorial Day donation to the veterans' home."

"Was your father a vet?"

He nodded.

"I'm sorry. Does he have Alzheimer's?"

"Yeah." He looked for a garbage can, found one, and threw away his cup, taking hers also.

"That's brutal."

They should get back to the cabin before someone recognized her.

"Luke?"

He stopped, and realized he'd walked out before her. Ten feet before her. She caught up with him, touched his arm. "Are you okay?"

The way she looked up at him, well . . . "It's just hard to

see him like that. He and I didn't always get along, and the last time we really spoke, it wasn't friendly. I left town and didn't come back for about five years, and by then, he'd gotten bad. He has some good days, but . . ."

He wasn't sure why she was so easy to talk to, but there she was, staring up at him, her glasses pushed up, compassion in her eyes. "But you wish you could go back, change the past. Redo your last moment."

He swallowed, shoved his hands into his jean pockets. Stared at the frothy river. "I was high on Vicodin one night. I was living in the Silver Stream in our backyard. My mother saw me leaving on my bike, and got my pop. We had a fight, and I . . ." He shook his head, not sure at all why he was letting her so far into his world. She said nothing, just waited.

"I put him in the hospital."

She drew in a breath.

"I didn't know what I was doing. It was the PTSD in me, but that wasn't an excuse. I hopped on my bike and left town. Didn't stop until I reached Nashville, then I checked myself into rehab."

"You took care of it."

"Yeah. Sort of. I had to work it out of my system, so I got a job as a wildland firefighter. Ended up in Big Sky country, working for an outfit out of Ember, Montana, called the Jude County Hotshots. It only took a summer of fighting fires for me to realize I loved the solitude of the woods. So, I got a degree in forestry, and by the time I returned . . . it was too late." He shook his head. "Dad was gone."

No, *Oh Luke*, with pity in her voice. Just her staring at him, all that softness in her eyes.

He wanted it to go away. Didn't want to be the guy who'd just—somehow—opened up his chest right here in the middle of the park for a girl he barely knew.

More than that, he wanted to kiss her. Wanted to wrap his hand around the back of her neck and pull her to him, to release the emotions still swilling in his chest.

But it was just adrenaline. Just the longing to shake away the intimacy of his story with something physical.

And she was MacKenzie Grace, superstar, so far out of his league it should blind him. Not to mention her being a trained actress. Who knew but there she was, smelling good and playing a role.

But wow, she was good at it. Any more of this and she'd have him confessing all manner of secrets.

He found his voice, and a cool smile. "So now, I visit him once a week and hope that he hears me."

"I'm sure he does."

He shrugged. "It doesn't matter. I can't turn back time and tell him I'm finally trying to be the guy he hoped I'd be." He turned away, walking back to Main Street. He didn't wait for her to catch up until he reached the monument. He turned, then, and saw her standing at the announcement board.

"What are you doing?"

"Did you know they have karaoke at Clyde's Roadhouse on Thursdays?"

"We're not going to Clyde's."

"Why not? I've walked around town all day without a soul recognizing me. We'll be in a dimly lit bar." She came toward him. "C'mon. Please? I sing a mean rendition of '*Sweet Home Alabama*.'"

He stared at her. "Who are you?"

She looped her arm through his. "Tonight? I'm your cousin Fanny, from . . ." She paused, and when she spoke again, it emerged with an Australian accent. "Down under."

Shoot, a guy could probably lose his heart to a girl like Fanny.

Chapter Six

KENZIE HAD FORGOTTEN WHAT IT FELT LIKE TO HAVE FUN. Real fun. Not the kind for charity events when the cameras might find the perfect shot for *People* magazine, or even on some remote beach in the Caribbean where, yes, cameras might find her there too, and a gossip rag could scrutinize every inch of her body.

This was the kind of fun she'd forgotten, the kind normal people experienced.

The kind she needed after a week—no, make it six years —of being imprisoned by her fame.

But she'd escaped her fame here. A wayward glance at her might peg her as a tourist from Nashville, visiting her cousin Luke, or worse, from up there in them hills, thanks to her black Guns and Roses T-shirt and a pair of Levi's Luke had loaned her, hitched tight at the waist with her alligator belt.

Yes, tucked in this Roadhouse, sitting at a table in the corner, the smell of microbrew and deep-fried mozzarella sticks in the air, she began to remember what freedom—real fun—tasted like. From the twang of a Brad Paisley imitator crooning on the far stage, to the audience singing along to "I'm Still a Guy."

Now, as Luke sat beside her, she barely recognized the man who a week ago acted like some sort of Blue Ridge grizzly, fangs out.

He sat with his back in the corner so he could see the room, she guessed, wearing a black T-shirt that proved he still had his military physique, nursing a coke and singing, "'I'll pour out my heart . . . hold your hand in the car . . . write a love song that makes you cry.'"

Sure, she'd noticed him at night when he got home and hid out in the Air Stream. Or at the stove, cooking another deer hamburger, the way he filled out his flannel shirt with those amazing shoulders, his strong legs in a pair of Levi's. Noticed his limp, too, but hadn't wanted to ask.

He had the Alexander good looks—molten gold hair, long, that curled behind his ears, a hint of stubble flecked with cedar in the morning. And those eyes.

Those green eyes could hold her hostage without protest.

But they hadn't truly undone her until today. Until Luke let her peek inside, see the story behind all that intensity. His honesty today had unraveled her—she'd forgotten that kind of honesty, those sweet, private places of a man's heart. Then again, Hollywood wasn't a place for honesty, for authenticity.

For men like Luke.

Which meant she shouldn't be enjoying this escape, this never-never-land friendship quite so much. But what was a girl to do when, like now, he glanced at her with those lethal eyes?

They could so easily find her heart, tug at the loneliness she'd managed to dodge since Nils left.

She'd found that loneliness again this week, pattering around Luke's house, seeing his family in the pictures, suddenly missing hers. She could feel the nudge growing, the one that said that in two measly hours, she could be home, sitting in her mother's kitchen, wolfing down a chicken fried steak. And never mind calling—her folks hadn't had a telephone since the phone company cut it off that year Papa lost his job and Mama didn't know how to write more than her name.

But if Kenzie showed up in her hometown, a pinprick on the map that had her face on the "Welcome to Harmony" sign, it would only bring the press to her backyard. Uncovering her secrets.

Secrets. *"I'm just tired of hiding. Tired of lying. And the worst part is, I'm afraid Lorenzo and his gang haven't forgotten and they're going to show up here and hurt the people I love."* She tried to erase the eavesdropped words she'd overheard from Luke today, but they wouldn't let go. Not even inside the smoky honky-tonk, with the entire audience shouting, "I'm still a guy."

Tired of lying.

Tired of hiding.

Hurt the people I love.

Like his father.

The crowd erupted as the song ended, and the crooner on the stage, a man wearing a backwards UT baseball cap over his tousled dark hair, handed the mic back to the MC. He waved to the audience, flexing as he walked off the stage.

The MC was a petite waitress with short red hair. "Who wants to come up here and sing us a little Faith Hill or Carrie Underwood?"

Kenzie glanced at Luke but he met her gaze and shook his head. "You promised, Fanny."

He was still calling her by her Aussie name. Okay, she liked it.

"C'mon, Luke. Who's going to recognize me? I look like Redneck Girl—I don't even recognize myself."

73

Not exactly the truth, but he didn't have to know that.

He leaned over to her, talked above the crowd. "I'm not sure why I agreed to this, but if you have to sing, you can howl to the moon when we get home." He winked.

Oh, his wink could turn her to warm grits.

Greg shouldn't have sounded quite so smug today when she called him, told him that yes, she was fine out here in east Tennessee. But the cops in LA had interviewed everyone she'd ever known, practically—house staff, delivery men, even her manicurist, and apparently they weren't getting any closer to a lead. Greg had suggested she might be stuck here for the entire summer.

Yes, she probably should have reacted with more protest.

The MC got a fresh victim who cued up a Brooks and Dunn song. Around her, tables emptied as dancers got up, pushed back tables.

"C'mon, Luke! Bring your gal up here."

She followed the voice and saw a broad-shouldered, shaggy-faced man who looked like he carved logs with a chainsaw for a living gesturing across the room.

Luke lifted his hand. "I'm good, Rog! No dancing for me—"

But two ladies pulled him up. "Dance, Luke!" The redheaded MC shoved him toward Kenzie.

"Sorry."

But she was on her feet. "Fear not. I know how to two-step."

He raised an eyebrow and reached for her hand. It closed around hers, soft, protective.

"I apologize already for your feet," he said as he brought her to the floor and wound her into his arms.

He smelled good—soap, and some sort of cologne. Or the fragrance of the freshener from today's laundry. She slid her hand onto his shoulder, found it solid. He stood a good five inches taller than her and, when she looked up, she found his gaze on her. "Try not to be conspicuous," he said.

"You lead, I'll follow."

He seemed impressed as he two-stepped her around the dance floor. "They have a lot of honky-tonks in LA?"

She debated. But he'd shown her a piece of his past, so, "I grew up in North Carolina."

He raised an eyebrow.

"In a little town over the state line called Honeysuckle."

"I've been there. Don't blink—"

"Or you'll miss it, I know."

He grinned. Oh boy. Yes, she might be in a heap of trouble if she stayed here another month.

He turned her out, back in, and as the song ended, dipped her.

Really. *Oh boy.*

They found their way back to the seat as a Miranda Lambert song cued up.

"If you're from North Carolina, why didn't you just go hide there?"

She drained the last of her beer. "Because if I showed up in my hometown, someone would alert the press, and the last thing I need is an overzealous reporter scaring my parents. They wouldn't know what to do."

He frowned.

Here she went. A little truth. "My parents are learning-disabled. They don't read, and for most of my life, we lived off welfare."

Just the slightest frown creased his face.

"I am their only child, and spent most of my life taking care of them. I long ago set up a fund for them—they'll never have to work again, even if my father continues to take in cars for repair in our barn."

She knew he wanted to know so, "I tested quite high in my IQ."

"I wasn't thinking—"

"Of course you were. But that's okay. I grew up with people underestimating me, mocking me, and most of all mocking my parents. I won't have that happen on a national scale. So no, I'm not going home."

Luke swallowed. "I'm sorry . . ."

Poor man, the protector in him simply did not know what to do with that information.

"They're my parents. I love them—"

He touched her arm, looked past her. "Shh."

She made to turn around but he tightened his hold. "What?"

"It's Candy. She's at the bar."

"Candy?"

"From Nashville? The *Parade*?"

"What is she still doing here?" She wanted to turn, but his breathing had increased, his expression tight.

As if, right before her eyes, he'd morphed into a soldier. The kind who had spent time in a Mexican prison camp. The kind who intended to escape this roadhouse, without casualties.

"Let's go. Keep it casual and stay behind me until you get to the door."

Shoot. Fun over. She got up, let him take her hand again. He moved her behind him, and she ducked her head as he weaved around the tables to the exit.

She felt as if she were back in one of her movies, and ducked down, ready to roll, to hide behind a table.

"What in Sam Hill are you doing?"

"Sneaking?"

"Just get outside." He opened the door for her and nudged her outside. The cool air smelled fresh and healing after the cloister of the bar. Overhead, the night sprinkled stars like white paint flung onto a canvas.

"Do you think she saw us?"

He unlocked his truck door, and she slid into the cab. "I don't know. Would you notice a woman duck-walking her way out of a crowded bar?"

"Listen, I learned some pretty stealthy moves over the past six years. Hayes 006 can keep up with Bourne any day."

She saw a grin, but he didn't look at her as he backed up. "You and Matt Damon have spy class together?"

"Matt learned everything he knows from me."

"I'm sure he did, Fanny." He pulled out onto the highway.

"My real name is MacKenzie Grace Talmadge." And for the first time since she left for college, she let her drawl run free.

"Wow, you are Southern."

She reached for her seat belt. "I was right at home back there, believe me. We don't have any honky-tonks in LA. That was fun. Probably more fun than I've had in a long time. And I haven't sung karaoke since college. I really wanted to sing."

"Really?"

"I love to sing. For a while, wanted to be in musical theater. I did Chicago at Duke, played Roxie Hart."

"What happened?"

"I decided to be in the movies instead. I thought I could make a bigger imprint on the world if I shot for the stars."

"And, have you?"

She wasn't sure— "Are you mocking me?"

"Why would I mock you?"

"Because I'm . . . well, I'm Hayes O'Brien 006. I haven't really saved the world. Just pretended to."

"Funny, I thought Hayes was a character. I thought you were MacKenzie Grace, actress and indie film producer."

"You know about my indie film?"

He pulled off the highway, onto a side road. The moon transformed it to a silver ribbon.

"Greg told me about it. Said you were trying to raise money."

"I need a backer or two. I used all my personal funds for shooting and now that it's in the can, it needs to be edited, not to mention distributed. I'm out of cash."

"Why an indie film?"

She leaned back on the seat, rubbed her arm. Maybe she shouldn't have taken off the sling for tonight. "While I was filming Lethal Target, we went to Patong, Thailand. Our hotel was inhabited by an inordinate amount of Americans. Especially men. So I asked my translator about it."

"And?"

"They were there on vacation. To hire the local little girls and boys for . . . for . . ."

His face was suddenly grim. "I got it."

"I couldn't believe it, so I started doing some research. UNICEF estimates that there are over two million children trapped in the commercial sex trade. Parents in Malaysia and Thailand—and too many other countries—sell their children to pay off debt, or even in the belief that they will live a better life. Imagine selling your own child, or even giving them to an uncle or aunt you trust in a big city only to find out they've been sold and sent to Saudi Arabia."

He met her eyes. "I had no idea."

"Neither did I. They say that there are more slaves worldwide today than there were during the time of slavery in America. But nobody really knows about it. So I made an indie film in hopes of distributing it in America. Maybe drum up awareness, even support to fight it.

"I couldn't escape the plight of those kids. It gnawed at

me. I know what it's like to feel trapped, to feel like no matter what you do, you'll never have a better life."

His voice was quiet, far away. "To lie there, night after night, listening to your heartbeat, trying to figure out how to escape."

"The slow despair that seeps in at the helplessness—"

"Of believing that this is it. Your life is over."

She drew in her breath. Stared at him. "Yes."

He didn't look at her. His hands were white on the steering wheel. He slowed and pulled into a park. A lake lay before them, glistening and filled with stars.

He said nothing as he pulled up and stopped. Finally, "I was held captive for six months in a Mexican prison camp."

She slid her hand over his arm, kept her voice soft. "Coop told me."

A muscle tightened in his jaw. "Yeah, well you can find it on a Google search. It's not a secret."

"I didn't Google you, Luke. Why were you there?"

He glanced at her, what looked like gratefulness in his eyes. "I was in a special unit, and we were working with the DEA, trying to shut down the traffic of drugs over the Arizona border. Unfortunately, a buddy and I were captured during a raid, and held."

His arm tensed under her grip.

"How'd you get away?"

He stared out at the lake. "A kid helped us. Luis. He was about ten years old, and was the son of one of the guards. He liked to practice his English on us. After a while, he started slipping us food. When it came time for us to be rescued, the SEALs used him to get information to us. They also planted a couple grenades in a bag of potatoes. He was supposed to deliver them, but something happened, and one of them went off. The entire camp went crazy. The team escaped, but not without casualties."

"Luis."

"And my buddy Darrin. He got shot during the escape—We left him with the other grenade."

His jaw tightened on his last words.

"Luke."

"No one outside of classified personnel knows how we escaped—it would put the SEAL team in jeopardy. They think we were alone."

Oh. "I won't tell a soul."

He put his hand to his chest. "They were closing in on our position, and there was no time. We were being overrun, and they couldn't carry both of us. So—"He shook his head. "He stayed and sacrificed himself so we could run under the cover of the explosion."

He closed his eyes. "Aw, shoot. I didn't mean to destroy our evening."

Oh, Luke. He hadn't destroyed anything. If anything, he'd made it golden. "Were you injured?"

He drew in a breath. "They busted up my leg pretty good. I could barely walk. I had to have my knee replaced, spent about a year in rehab."

"That's how you got hooked on Vicodin."

He nodded.

"And the memory of your friend made taking them a good idea."

"I've been dying to tell someone—the world—since we left. Tell them how Darrin was a hero, how he sacrificed himself so I could be free." He looked at her then, his eyes shiny. "What is it about you, Fanny? I can't shut up around you."

She smiled then, a warmth in her chest that came from the places inside that wanted to wrap her arms around him, to tuck him to herself. "I have to confess, I heard you today when you were talking to your dad. Who are you afraid will find you?"

"The men who took us. They have long arms, and I've long feared they'd find me here, in Tennessee."

"Which is why you live so deep in the woods."

"Off the grid."

"I'd call it away from humanity."

He lifted a shoulder.

She wasn't an idiot. Guilt put a hand between relationships. And Luke wore his guilt, his shame in his eyes like a No Trespassing sign.

"Thank you for letting me invade your world."

"If only it had plumbing, huh?" But his gaze told her, for the first time, that perhaps he didn't mind so much.

Perhaps he liked having her around.

Yeah, well, she liked being here.

Here, she could forget her failures, forget Nils and his new lead, forget the pile of scripts back at the cabin, forget her sinking career, the fact she was broke. Or that someone was trying to kill her.

Here she could be Fanny from Australia. Or even Kenzie Talmadge, honky-tonk gal. "I'm getting used to the throne."

He smiled and it turned her inside out, made her feel like honey. She watched the moon dapple the lake with gold. "Why are we here?"

He seemed to startle, as if he'd forgotten he'd driven her to a lake, out in the middle of nowhere with stars sprinkled across the surface, the fragrance of the night stirring the sycamore trees.

"You said you wanted to sing."

"Here?"

He got out, walked around the truck. Opened her door. "Belt it out, MacKenzie Grace."

81

She laughed and let him help her from the truck. "I don't have any music."

He was standing so close to her, she could smell him, intoxicating and delicious.

"Aw, if anyone could make her own music, it's you, Fan."

So that's where Greg got his country charm. Her face heated, but she couldn't hide a smile.

Thankfully, he moved away, stalking toward a picnic table. "Over here. Your own stage."

"I am not singing—"

He turned and came back at her, almost like he might be charging, and without a skip, scooped her up in his arms. "Luke—What—?"

He strode over to the table and stood her on it. "Sing, Fanny."

"Uh . . . well . . ."

"Sing for me."

"Oh, please—"

But grinning up at her like he was, the moon in his eyes, what was a girl to do?

Here went nothing. "Bmm . . . Bmm . . . Bm . . . Bmm . . . Bmm . . . Bm . . . 'When the night has come . . . And the land is dark . . . And the moon is the only light we'll see . . .'"

She looked down at him, and because he was grinning, she grabbed his hand, pulled him up. "'No . . . I won't be afraid . . . No I won't be afraid . . . Just as long as you stand, stand by me.'"

She shoved her fake microphone/closed fist at him. Hoping.

And then he did it. Let loose with a tenor that reverberated right through her, and into the night.

"'Oh, darlin', darlin' . . .'"

Oh, darlin' was right. She let him take the lead, let his

voice reverberate across the lake, then joined him in the next verse.

But she didn't expect it when, at the next chorus, he curled a hand around her waist and pulled her into a dance. Nothing fancy, just close and sweet and fun as he lowered his voice into her ear and sang the words over and over. "'Stand by me—'"

Yes.

And then, she couldn't help it. Not with the moon cajoling her, the night air sweet with the scent of spring. She'd escaped herself anyway, for now, so she wound her arms around his neck and pulled herself close. And when he met her eyes, she didn't stop to think.

She kissed him.

He tasted sweet, his lips soft, and for a second, unmoving.

And then, blessed relief, he kissed her back. Moving his hands up to tangle in her hair as he came alive and practically inhaled her. Like a long drink of water, as if so thirsty he couldn't let her go. He pulled her closer, angled his head down, and kissed her like he meant it.

Her too. Because in this magical pocket of star-strewn east Tennessee, she saw the girl she had been, the girl she wanted to be. The girl she'd forgotten.

More than that, she couldn't remember the last time she'd been held like this, or been kissed with such honesty. As if he needed her.

And for now, she needed him right back. She molded herself to him, let her fingers weave through his hair, relishing his strong arms around her, the last notes of their song still lingering in her head.

Luke. She may have even said his name as he pulled away, looked into her eyes, as if searching for something.

She gave him a soft smile, searching his eyes.

Suddenly, he jerked away from her, looking into the woods. "What was that?"

It rattled her. She had to hang on to his arm to keep from tumbling off the table as he whirled around, peering into the darkness of the parking lot. "Who's out there?" he yelled.

His tone whisked a chill through her. "What did you see?"

"I don't know. Something. A flash of light."

Oh no. Not out here. "Paparazzi?"

He looked at her, and his expression froze her. "That would be better than a gun, wouldn't it?"

Maybe. "I think . . . maybe—"

"Yes, let's go." He hopped off the table, reached up, and grabbed her around her waist.

Um, she'd been about to suggest he was just paranoid, but as he took her hand, pulling her toward the truck, she saw it too. A flicker of light, as if something shiny caught in the moonlight.

Could be a flash.

Or not.

She climbed into the truck, and he slammed the door behind her then stalked around to the other side. When he climbed in, just like that, he'd changed.

No more Southern boy charmer.

No more crooner.

Back to grizzly.

"This was a very bad idea," he said, running his hand over the back of the seat as he backed up then tore out of the lot. "A very bad idea."

Chapter Seven

THEY WEREN'T ALONE LAST NIGHT UNDER THE STARS, AND THE broken rhododendron proved it.

In the hazy light of the morning, one covered by too many clouds, Luke surveyed the area around the broken leaves, stems, looking for a useable footprint—at least to get the size and perhaps weight of their stalker.

In his worst nightmares, it belonged to Lorenzo, or one of his men. But then, most likely, he and Kenzie wouldn't be alive.

Or, if they were, they'd be suffering.

He stepped out of the enclave just beyond the parking lot. Yes, from here, the voyeur had a perfect view of the lake, the picnic table.

Of Luke holding Kenzie in his arms.

And if he let his mind linger there too long, he could see it too. Feel the way she reached up and pulled him close, the way she'd kissed him, her touch almost healing.

He had forgotten himself in the smells of her hair, the way she looked at him. Not like Ruthann, who always worried about him relapsing, or his father's vacant stare, so many secrets locked in his head. Not even like the women in town who regarded him as a hermit, odd.

Kenzie made him feel like someday he might be whole again.

Until the flash of light. It should have been accompanied by a thunderclap and maybe even a strike of heat through the heart, because it jolted him back to his senses.

Being with him would only get a woman hurt. Especially a woman like Kenzie who had already had a stalker on her six.

Luke strode back to his truck, refusing to remember the silences of their ride home, the one where he wanted to confess that with everything inside him he wanted to turn the truck south and head over the border. Or root around in the Silver Stream, hoping he might find a forgotten stash of Vicodin. Or simply pack up her belongings and ship her back to Greg.

In fact, that was exactly what he planned to do.

Luke climbed into the truck and motored back down the mountain to town. Thankfully, he'd left Kenzie at the cabin today, without wheels. He'd hated the look on her face as he'd driven away, but this was why he didn't let people get too close.

He could hardly do his job with her smile, her laughter in his head, noodling his brain. He was supposed to keep her safe.

At this rate, he'd get her killed.

Go, Luke. Run. Tell my wife that I love her.

Darrin's voice knew just how to haunt him. Luke gripped the wheel, but the smells of his own fear, blood, the dank humidity of the jungle, could rise up like a vine to choke him when the memories broke free.

Sweat broke out down his spine.

He cracked his window. Saw Luis running toward him, a potato bag over his shoulder, grinning. One second there, the next—

He drew in long breaths of the cool air. Maybe he should pull over.

Music. He needed music. He turned on the radio. Brad Paisley came on, singing about fishing.

We have to go, Luke. Now!

He'd bit his lip. He could taste blood on his tongue as he whisked it away.

He turned off the music.

Listened to his heartbeat as he drove past his office and into town.

He found himself at the parking lot of the residence center, staring at the building.

Overhead, the blue sky had bled out into a whitish gray, mourning the loss of the sun behind the clouds. He could smell rain. The mighty Watauga River rumbled in the distance, where it cut through the lawn.

What he wouldn't give for five more minutes with his father. The father who had chased him down too many nights over at Red's Bar, or the one who had shoved him into his car, forced him to attend PT. The father who had fought his own private battle with fear and battle fatigue from his tour in Vietnam and won. How had he escaped the demons?

How had he escaped the loneliness?

Luke leaned his head against the steering wheel. Perhaps it was enough to just sit out here. Maybe he could find a stillness inside the whirr of his head.

"Luke?" He looked up, found Missy standing at his door, a sweater over her arm, dressed in her pink nurse's uniform. "Are you okay?"

87

He knew her from the days when she sat in the third pew from the front with her family. She'd married Harley Fink and had two elementary-age children, but when she looked at him, he still saw the girl with the long blonde hair, the shy smile, still remembered trying to conjure up the words to ask her out.

"I . . ."

"You know, sometimes I have to sit here too, and find the courage to go inside. It's hard to see so many of the people we love fading before our eyes."

Yes.

"But you know, I have this sense that they still know what is going on. I think they see more than they let on."

He nodded, hating how his eyes burned.

"It must be hard to be trapped inside your body, unable to speak the words you know you could give to others. Or reach out and hold a hand." She switched her sweater to her other arm. "But every once in a while . . ."

She looked past him, a smile on her face. "You know the other day, I was adjusting your father's bed, and just for a second, he looked at me. Like he did from the pulpit—you know how he'd look at the audience, and he'd meet your eyes, and you thought maybe he knew your sins?"

Luke could smile at that. "I thought that was just me he could do that to."

"Oh no. He had powers to make me confess then and there. But kindness too. Grace."

"That was my dad."

"That *is* your dad. He's still there. He's just locked away in his body and mind. But God hasn't abandoned him. I have to believe that God knows exactly what your dad is thinking, what he's going through. And every once in a while, he gives us all a glimpse that your dad is still there."

"Alzheimer's is stripping everything that he was—that he *is* away from him."

"No it's not. He's still the same man of character."

He looked away. Tightened his jaw. "I miss him."

"I know you do." Her voice softened. "And that's how it's supposed to be. We're supposed to be entwined in each other's lives so much that we hold each other up, that we embed our impression upon them. I remember your dad cheering at your football games, and those days he wheeled you into the hospital for PT. I remember him asking us to pray for you when you disappeared in Mexico. Of course you miss him. But you wouldn't want it the other way, would you? To not have that raw place inside, right? And the fact is, Luke, you are so much like him—you have that same intensity, that same drive. He left his impression on you—and now you long for it."

He wanted to reach up, actually rub his chest where it burned.

"That raw place is a reminder that you were loved, and that you know how to love back. It's a good thing." She tapped his truck, almost like patting his shoulder. "He needs you now to do the remembering for him. Only your love can draw him out of that dark place where he's trapped."

She offered him a final smile then went into the building.

He wanted to believe her. Really. But she hadn't been there to witness the flameout of their relationship. Luke couldn't bear the thought that it might be *that* moment permanently imprinted in his father's memory.

Too many demons still lurked from his ordeal in Mexico, and he had no idea how to escape them. Maybe he never would.

And, as if to confirm, just as he put his truck into reverse, a white Fiat pulled up behind him, blocking him in.

He stuck his head out the window. "Hey!"

The door opened and one sleek leg, then another slid out. Candy.

"Howdy, Luke. Feel free to stay in the truck. I was just on my way to your office to deliver this." She walked up to him holding a bulky manila envelope.

"I already saw the *Parade.* Excellent reporting, Candy. I'm not sure why you even bothered to interview me."

"Did we have an interview? Couldn't tell."

He began to open the envelope.

"Oh, it can wait until you get to the office." She winked at him. "Call me."

Right.

He threw the envelope onto the seat, watched her pull away. Glanced back at the envelope. It looked like it contained a book.

Dark Secrets, no doubt.

Yes, it could definitely wait.

He pulled out of the lot and headed toward the office. He'd stop by to see Dad after he buried himself in work for a while, let the voices subside.

Cooper sat at his desk, glancing up as Luke walked in, shrugged off his jacket, and hung it on the hook.

"You okay? You look like you ate a badger for breakfast."

"Fine." Luke pulled out his chair. He had a stack of camping permits to log in and approve, and a request for a fire prevention demonstration over at Sycamore Shoals Elementary. He'd hand that one off to Coop.

Firing up his laptop, he clicked over to e-mail. Debated writing to Greg. Closed the e-mail.

Maybe they could both leave. Just, well, just *vanish* for a while. He could take her hiking along the Appalachian Trail. He couldn't help a smile at the sight of her in a pair of hiking boots and a flannel shirt.

Sure she grew up in North Carolina. He wanted to believe her. Liked the idea of knowing her secrets—Hayes 006, Southern, small-town girl.

"Like to kill me, trying to track you down."

He stilled and looked up. Ruthann had a hand on her hip, the other holding with an iron grip to Trevor's jacket collar. The kid was trying to twist away from her, without luck. "Do you ever charge your cell phone?"

He hadn't even looked at it the past two days. "Sorry, Sis."

"Trevor, settle down, you're not going anywhere. Listen, I finally drove out to your place and surprise, surprise, I found a woman there."

As if on cue—and he supposed she knew stage timing— Kenzie breezed into the office wearing his jean jacket, the sleeves rolled up. She had her hair braided in two long ropes and a baseball cap atop her head. She looked almost sheepish as she glanced at him.

As if she might be a renegade.

"Hey, Luke."

"Hi . . ." He wasn't sure what name she might be going by today.

Ruthann raised an eyebrow, accusing. "Celinda told me how you rescued her this weekend when her car broke down on Roan Mountain. I gave her a lift into town to pick it up."

"Oh, uh . . ." He looked at, well, Celinda. "I called the shop. They said it wouldn't be ready until . . ." When? Tomorrow? He might be able to get her on a plane by then. "Later today. Maybe tomorrow."

"Perfect," Ruthann said. "Then you can bring her to the Watauga Fort Muster tonight."

He closed his eyes.

"Luke, c'mon. You never go, and you know it's Rollie's big event."

Ruthann turned to Kenzie. "My husband plays the

91

Reverend Samuel Doak. The muster reenacts a pre-battle prayer that took place here in 1790, when frontiersmen from our area gathered right before their victory on King's Mountain in South Carolina against British loyalists. All the deacons and elders in town take turn leading the muster prayer—this is our church's week, and we have a church family potluck tonight."

"Ruthann—"

"Our father used to play the reverend. It's tradition for our family to be involved."

Perfect. And one look at Kenzie told him that she'd eaten up Ruthann's words like a macaroni casserole.

"No."

"We'll be there."

He stared at her. Kenzie smiled at him, those eyes that last night had made him do stupid, out of his body things. Like kiss her. Like forget that there might be someone trying to hurt her. And him. Definitely him. And everyone he loved.

"Ke-Celinda. I think your car might be—"

"For your sister, Luke? I think I can stick around." She turned to Ruthann. "Thank you for the invitation."

Ruthann leaned over and patted his cheek. "Excellent." She turned to Kenzie. "Can I drop you somewhere?"

"How about the coffee shop?"

Of course.

"Celinda—" he said as she turned to follow Ruthann. "A word?"

She glanced at Ruthann. "I'll be right there."

Kenzie still had the smile as she returned to Luke, but she glanced at Cooper and cut her voice low. "I didn't know what to do. She showed up at the cabin, and I had to think fast."

She sounded truly apologetic, and he just couldn't tell her about the voyeur until he knew more. Still, "I'm not sure this is such a good idea."

"It's your sister. Or is that the problem? You don't want me to meet her."

"I don't want her to recognize you."

Kenzie added a twang to her drawl. "Why, Lukie, I'm just here for the muster, right?"

"It's not funny." But she looked so cute, he fought a smile.

Hers, however, dimmed. "No one will recognize me, Luke. Everything is going to be just fine. I'll be in the park when you're ready to go home."

He wanted to catch her, to pull her to himself, but she slipped out into the parking lot and he saw her laughing as she climbed into the passenger seat.

Oh boy.

But maybe she was right. If Ruthann didn't recognize her

. . .

Maybe the trampling of the bushes had been a couple having their own private karaoke.

Maybe he'd simply overreacted to the fact that Kenzie had gotten under his skin and unraveled him. Made him realize he had something to lose.

"The muster, huh?" Coop said from across the room. "Celinda?"

"That's enough from you," Luke said as he reached for the manila envelope. For a second, it hovered over the trash. Then he ran his thumb under the flap.

Indeed, *Dark Secrets* slipped out onto his desk. That, and an envelope.

He pulled it out, opened it.

Froze.

Pictures of him and Kenzie. At the Roadhouse, at the park. On the picnic table.

In each other's arms.

And a yellow Post-it note on the last one, over their lip-lock.

93

Actress MacKenzie Grace Spotted in East Tennessee in Arms of Local So-Called Hero.

And below that, Candy had scribbled,

Your interview for my silence. Just how much do you want to keep your secret?

Chapter Eight

KENZIE EMBRACED HER ROLE AS SOUTHERN FRONTIERSWOMAN. She wasn't sure what her character's name might be—Celinda didn't feel historical enough, and dressed in a long skirt, a prairie blouse, her hair pulled back in a bonnet, she felt a little like a Laura. Or a Mary. Or a Carrie. All she needed was Pa and her horse Bunny to complete the portrait drawn in the grassy muster grounds of Fort Watauga. When she'd goaded Luke into attending—and yes, goaded seemed the appropriate word after the way he showed up, the only thundercloud to a gorgeous day—she didn't imagine that *she'd* be mustered into playing an extra for the enactment.

Of course, her sole duty was to stand in the background holding a pie, courtesy of Ruthann's picnic basket. Still, watching the preacher pray over the assembled musters swept her back into an age when life felt simpler. Love your family. Fight for your country. Cling to your faith.

She glanced at Luke, seated on a picnic table, his feet on the bench, watching her. If anyone embodied loving his family, or fighting for his country . . .

And maybe they both needed to cling to their faith a bit

more. What had the preacher said? Something about standing firm in the faith, because without faith, you had nothing solid beneath you.

She stared at the pie, the smells of the meringue on top of the banana cream nearly ready to topple her over, or make her run for the hills. A homemade touch to the event, provided by a couple of the actors.

People reliving traditions. Holding on to their roots, their values. It defined them, gave their lives stability, even identity.

She'd forgotten the value of standing firm. In her identity. In her faith.

The preacher was still praying, and she could barely make out his words across the mass of men dressed in breeches and leather jackets and holding ancient—probably replica —muskets.

"So, Lord, we beseech your favor upon our company as we face the British sympathizers. Help us be bold and to hold fast to what we believe and what we are fighting for. Our homes. Our families. Our glorious tomorrow as a nation, and the freedom to worship our Creator and live our lives without tyranny." He held up his hands, and the murmur of "Amen" traveled through the crowd.

Amen.

Across the horizon, the sun streamed across the Watauga and through the yellow buckeye trees, a glorious stream of gold into the late afternoon as the crowd erupted into a rousing rendition of "The Battle Hymn of the Republic." "'Mine eyes have seen the glory of the coming of the Lord . . .'" She felt pretty sure the old Southern hymn wasn't historically accurate to the time period, but it felt right to sing it.

"'His truth is marching on . . .'"

The crowd dispersed as they sang, and Ruthann waved to

her from the sidelines. She released Trevor's hand and he ran through the crowd to his father, who scooped the little frontier boy into his arms.

He squealed with delight as his father flung him over his shoulder and trotted up to the picnic table where Luke was helping Ruthann lay a cloth and unload the basket.

"Thank you for the pie prop," Kenzie said as she handed it back to Ruthann. "I nearly licked it so I could have the entire thing."

Ruthann laughed. "That sounds like something Luke would have done a few years ago."

Kenzie glanced at him to see if he'd respond, but he ignored them.

"You went to a lot of work here. Fried chicken, potato salad, biscuits." She could nearly taste the multitude of Sunday afternoon potlucks back in Harmony as Ruthann piled the containers on the table.

"Last year I tried sushi, and my entire family said they'd never attend again. So, it's back to traditions. Apparently, raw tuna is not appropriate muster food."

You should come to LA and try out the sushimi at—Oops. The words nearly broached her lips, but she bit them back.

Today, right now, she was still Celinda.

But suddenly, she didn't want to be. The anonymity of being tucked away with this community had raised a desire to be herself—not MacKenzie Grace, aka Hayes 006, but Kenzie, the girl who'd played softball and waited tables down at the Firelight Grill on Saturday nights. She wanted to be the girl who dreamed of a home and children, of having a Trevor tussling in his father's arms.

Of having a husband who would know her and give her an intimate smile across a crowded lawn of muster-ers.

She glanced at Luke.

Yes, he was looking at her. But no intimate smile. In fact,

his eyes could probably bore right through her, turn her to fire. She frowned at him, and he turned away.

"He's in a stellar mood today, as usual," Ruthann said. "I'm not sure why I insist he join us at family events. I guess I keep hoping that someday he'll forgive himself and come back to us."

"Forgive himself?"

Ruthann shook her head, gave her what seemed a forced smile. "Sorry. Personal family stuff. Luke carries around a lot of shame for something that we all forgave him for long ago, and he thinks we don't want him around. He doesn't seem to notice that we keep inviting him to family events and that Trevor adores him. I wish he'd get it through his thick head that it's okay to have people care about you—that sometimes you let each other down. But you don't give up on each other. You don't stop believing the best in them."

She handed Kenzie a stack of paper plates. "Fact is, we know Luke, and the kind of man he is, and one—or two—mistakes doesn't change that. He doesn't need to prove himself to the people who love him."

"I don't know. It's the people who you love who you want to impress the most." Kenzie wasn't sure where the words came from, but Ruthann looked up at her.

Considered her for a moment. Then, "I suppose it is. Funny paradox."

She waved to her husband, who had taken out a football from their gear and begun throwing it to Trevor, then to Luke. He was catching it and tossing it back, his face stoic.

"Time to eat!"

Luke didn't look at her as he strode over to the table. He slid in opposite her and reached for the potato salad.

Ruthann slapped at his hand. "Hello? Not until we say grace."

Luke ground his jaw as Kenzie bowed her head.

He ate his food like he might be on death row, not meeting her eyes as Ruthann asked her about her life. Kenzie pulled from her past, created a persona from the person she'd been.

The person she might like to be.

"I live in North Carolina, just down the street from my parents. I help run the local theater, and . . ." She glanced at Luke. "Sometimes I sing karaoke down at the local blues joint."

Shoot. Not even this got a rise from him.

What had happened to the version of Luke she'd met last night, the one crooning out "Stand By Me"? The one who'd taken her into his arms, who'd kissed her like . . .

Like he'd meant it.

Oh, she had let her overactive imagination run away with her. They were playacting—she had to remember that. And he'd just gotten into character a bit too much. Whatever had snapped him back to his senses had managed to turn him back into Grizzly Adams.

Maybe she didn't belong here.

Ruthann scooped her up a piece of banana cream pie. Kenzie stared at it, the bananas leaking out onto the plate.

But oh, she wanted to.

She picked up her fork, hating how she'd so easily let the charm of Normandy, her surreal life in the woods, woo her into believing that she could have something that didn't belong to her.

Like Luke.

Like a simpler life.

Family. Home. Faith.

Faith.

She hadn't given a lot of thought to faith, not recently, but that came with the package, didn't it? The life she'd left behind, the one she longed for, also included the lessons she'd learned in the polished pew of First Baptist of Harmony.

She'd left Harmony, her faith intact, her sense of identity unshaken. Ten years later, too many compromises made her turn around. How had she gotten so off track?

She'd lost herself, just like Luke, and was caught in the cycle of trying to prove herself to . . . well, herself. And the people she loved.

But even that had failed. No wonder she loved Normandy. Here, she could escape.

Just like Luke did, in his cabin in the woods.

"Great dinner, Ruthann," Luke said as he finished off his Kool-Aid. For the first time, he glanced at Kenzie. "Ready to go?"

Ruthann frowned at him. "What about the bonfire?"

He rolled his eyes.

Trevor, however, climbed down from his perch. "C'mon Unca Luke. Frow the football wif me."

For a moment, a softness entered Luke's eyes and the flash of it curled a warmth inside Kenzie.

"Okay, Trev. Ten minutes of catch. But we're not staying for the bonfire."

He slid out from the table.

Ruthann leaned over to her husband. "I have a blanket in the car. We'll pick a place by the fire and camp out there. He won't be able to leave."

Her husband began to get up but Kenzie caught him. "I'll get the blanket. I need to get my sweater anyway." She'd left it in Luke's cab when he picked her up.

She glanced at Luke, as she hiked back to the parking lot. She could see him, once upon a time, a rowdy football player, yelling commands to his teammates, or even as a soldier, solid, dependable.

She refused to let the image of the Navy Seals dragging him away from his buddy sear her mind. Still, it lodged there.

No wonder Luke struggled to live with himself. Kenzie had made poor choices, but none of them included leaving behind a friend to die.

She reached the truck. He hadn't locked it—apparently, one didn't need to in Normandy—and opened the door. Reached in for her sweater.

A manila envelope poked out from the pocket in the driver's side door. She'd seen it on his desk—bulky and sealed. Now, the top was ripped open, a jagged edge that evidenced a thumb running across the crease. And poking from the top, something that looked like—wait, a photo? Of her?

She glanced at Luke, still playing with Trevor, and couldn't help it.

She grabbed it and slid the contents out onto the seat. Her mouth dried as she stared at pictures of herself, of Luke, of their kiss.

As she read the note.

Candy. She'd seen them at the Roadhouse and recognized her. Worse, now she was blackmailing Luke into spilling his secrets.

No wonder the man couldn't look at Kenzie.

She wanted to climb into the cab and find the woman, to appear on her doorstep and demand reasons. Why reporters believed they could dig into . . . destroy the lives of others . . .

She shoved the pictures back into the envelope. Her hand shook as she considered hiding it, then she put it back into its place.

Candy wouldn't get her story. At least not the one about Luke.

Which meant that the fun and games had ended. Even if she wanted to stay, the show was over.

She pulled on the sweater and returned to the picnic table.

"Where's the blanket?" Ruthann was packing up lunch into the basket.

"I think Luke's right. My car is done in the shop, and I probably need to get on the road."

"Tonight?"

Kenzie forced a smile. "If I leave tonight, I can be home in a couple hours." Back to where she belonged.

Out of Luke's world.

She helped Ruthann pack up, ignoring her protests.

"But dusk is so beautiful this time of year, with the fireflies out, the sparks from the fire blowing into the sky. And you'll miss the storytellers."

Kenzie glanced at Luke. He'd just scooped up a pass and tossed it to Ruthann's husband, coming to relieve him.

She gave him a sad smile as he ran back. He frowned for a moment, then pasted on the fake Luke, the one she knew he fabricated for his sister.

The real Luke, the one she'd met last night, just might be gone forever.

"Ready to go?"

"Luke—" Ruthann started.

"Yes, please," Kenzie said softly.

He frowned again.

"The shop called. My car's ready. I should hit the road." All this lying—but it would be over soon, and she'd never see Ruthann again.

Another one of her many sins she'd just have to live with. The price she paid for her choices.

She didn't look at Luke as they hiked back to his truck. Behind her, she heard the town gathering for the bonfire, a bluegrass band warming up. The evening breeze, light and warm, stirred the smells of spring, fresh rhododendron, the trees now in bud.

She wanted to stay, warm her hands at the bonfire. Sing along.

Tuck herself into Luke's arms.

She slid into her side of the cab. Closed the door. Belted herself in.

He said nothing as he fired up the truck and backed out. Nothing as they drove down Main Street and then onto the highway toward the forest.

Her eyes burned.

But what could she say? *I found the pictures, I read Candy's ultimatum. You don't have to betray yourself for me, Luke.*

Yeah, that would go over well. She had no doubt he fully planned on complying with Candy's request.

"I'm leaving, Luke. Tonight. I would appreciate it if you could drive me to the airport in Knoxville. I'll get a hotel room and fly back to LA tomorrow."

After a moment of silence, she glanced at him. He stared straight ahead into the night.

No argument.

Of course.

She ground her jaw tight, fighting the way her throat closed, the way she wanted to press her hand to her mouth. She held on as his truck turned off to the rutted dirt road to his house.

This was for the best. She could nearly hear the words radiating off him. For the best. So she couldn't hurt him anymore.

They pulled up to the cabin and for a long moment, he just sat there, the motor running. She didn't want to move, didn't want to go inside and start packing.

Please.

Oh, she'd turned into a pitiful reflection of Hayes 006, who never pined for any man, who could handle a broken romance like tossing away an old pair of boots. Hayes 006 would not only track down Candy, but she'd exonerate Luke in the process.

The best Kenzie could do was leave town. Apparently she had become excellent at that maneuver.

She reached for the door latch, but in her movements, Luke came alive. He put a hand on her arm.

For a second, she thought he might have broken free of his snarl of emotions, his frustration—maybe even his anger. For a wild second she turned to him and hoped to find the man she'd seen last night.

The one who she dreamed might curl his hand around her neck and pull her to himself and kiss her. Make her forget her plans to leave, tell her that he needed her.

Just like she'd begun to need him.

But even as she looked at him, searched his face, her hopes dipped. He wasn't looking at her, but beyond her, towards the house, dimly lit by the spray of his headlights.

"Stay here."

His tone chilled her through. She watched him get out, walk to the door. Stand there.

No, she couldn't stay here—

"What is it?"

She left the door open and strode over just as he whirled around, put two hands on her shoulders. "Kenzie—"

"What it is, Luke?"

She sloughed off his hands and dodged him, stepping sideways enough to get a glimpse.

The odor should have stopped her, because it hit her then, full on. Stink. A skunk, its putrid odor, the tinny sharp smell of the blood that dropped from the carcass nailed to the door, and down to a puddle on the steps.

Now she put her hand to her mouth. She wouldn't

scream. Didn't have time for it, really, as Luke grabbed her arm and pulled her off the porch, packing her into the truck. "This time don't move."

He shut the door, used his key fob to lock her in. Then he disappeared into his Silver Stream. No more than two minutes later he emerged with what looked like a fully loaded backpack. He tossed it and two other bundles into the back of the truck, then climbed in beside her. Slamming the car into reverse, he backed up without a word and headed away from the cabin.

"What—Luke's what's going on?"

His knuckles turned white on the steering wheel. "You're not going anywhere, Kenzie. At least not without me." He turned his lights to dim, a phantom glow against the trees, and she guessed he'd practiced driving this road a few times with low visibility.

"In fact, it's time for us both to disappear."

Chapter Nine

A CHILL HUNG IN THE AIR, COATED THE BRISTLES OF THE LOW hanging Frasier firs, shivered the still-budding silver maples. An ethereal mist fingered its way through the valley of skeletal black birch and cascading green of Norway spruce and red cedar, the view from Luke's campsite. The water of a spring cascade hummed from the nearby river, and the air smelled of the late-season loam, the fragrance of dwarf-crested irises and yellow trout lilies and other ephemerals basking in the sunlight of the forest still leafing out.

Think, Luke, think. He stood at the cliff's edge overlooking a tumble of boulders that fell down to the valley, knotted with rhododendron, and tried to untangle the panic from the facts. Twilight swept through the folds of smoky blue mountains, the last whisper of pink and gold dying to the encroaching gray, the folds of darkness not long behind.

He had to get Kenzie to safety—back to Greg—while he figured out who had left the warning on his door.

But warning for whom? Kenzie, via her stalker? Or someone who'd finally tracked down Luke deep in the Cherokee forest?

Whatever the case, he had to disentangle her from himself and get her to someone who didn't have the wages of sin hanging over him.

Something, apparently, she'd finally figured out. Luke couldn't pinpoint exactly why her abrupt decision at the picnic to leave needled him, but he should probably be relieved.

Except, today, she'd seemed to have tucked herself so easily into his world, perched next to his sister, laughing, helping her set out the picnic. And in that moment, he'd seen it—the glimpse of the life he'd shoved so deep inside he'd forgotten he'd ever hoped for it. Family. Someone to share his life with.

Missy's words rushed back to him. *We're supposed to be entwined in each other's lives so much that we hold each other up, that we embed our impression upon them.*

But maybe not so entwined that he got the people he loved killed.

And besides, sometime after dinner, before he had a chance to really get in trouble by pulling her into his arms to nestle back against him under a bouquet of fireworks, she'd come to her senses.

I'm leaving, Luke. Tonight. I would appreciate it if you could drive me to the airport in Knoxville. I'll get a hotel room and fly back to LA tomorrow. Back to her life—her big life, the one she clearly wasn't going to sacrifice to join a hermit in the woods.

Except now, someone had left a warning, and she'd have to tie him up and leave him for dead before he'd simply leave her at some airport, waiting for someone to snatch her up.

Sorry, sugar, but she wasn't going anywhere without a full armada of protection.

Which left him at a sum-zero of options.

"We should be safe here, for now." He hadn't realized he'd

107

said it aloud until Kenzie came up to stand beside him. She'd said nothing as he'd thrown his backpack into the bed of the truck and driven them deep into the Appalachian forest, parking in a remote trickle of dirt, then hiking them another hour to this place.

Now, she wrapped her arms around herself, having put on the sweatshirt he'd offered her as the woods closed in around them, the air cooling as they trekked higher into the mountains. His shirt dwarfed her, and she suddenly appeared tiny and fragile in the glow of the fading sunlight. With one glance at him, her pretty eyes searching his for answers, she could take his breath away.

It was all he needed to awaken the sense of holding her in his arms, the taste of her—all forbidden longings he shook away. He fought the urge to reach out, pull her close, wrap himself around her to share his warmth.

He simply needed to keep her words—I'm leaving—in the forefront of his brain.

"Who do you think left it?" she asked now, referring to the sight of the bleeding skunk, freshly killed. The image seared his mind, the odor of death, the tinny scent of blood pooling on his deck still reeking in his nose.

And, he might never erase from his mind her hollow, whitened expression.

There it came again, the urge. He fisted his hands at his sides. "I don't know." The truth in his quiet, tenebrous words wound through him, turned him brittle. "But whoever it is, they won't find us tonight."

She made a soft noise, as if in agreement, then rubbed her hands over her arms, warding off the misty breath of the mountains. It would drop into the forties tonight, and he mentally winced at the fact that in his rush he'd forgotten a second sleeping bag.

"I'm sorry I didn't drive you to the airport, but I think this is safer, for now. Until we find out what's going on."

"The view is breathtaking." She stood for a moment longer, staring into the expanse of the mountains. "I forget, sometimes, the beauty of the Appalachians."

Watching her profile against the undulating, greening scoop of the valley, the magenta folds of dusk, her golden blonde hair tumbling down over her shoulders, loosened from their hike, her blue eyes wide with the luster of the forest—no he wouldn't forget, ever, what she'd brought to him. Even if the longing for it all would find him, haunt him long after the sense of her faded from the homestead.

No, he wouldn't forget.

"I found this view a couple years ago when I was out hunting for poachers."

"Poachers? What kind—elk?"

"Ginseng."

She made a sound of surprise. "Ginseng? Like the stuff they put in energy drinks?"

"That's the one. It's been grown here since the time of Daniel Boone. The locals call it Sweet Bubby, and you are legally allowed to harvest it with a permit. But poachers pull the wild plants up by the roots, raping them. We try and fight them with motion detectors and infrared, but way out here, we mark the plants with dye and silicon chips, and have to catch them after the fact. Unless I come out here occasionally and patrol. I caught two poachers last fall—stumbled on their campsite, littered with garbage and beer bottles and found them packing out over a thousand ginseng roots, about fifteen pounds worth. At the time, ginseng was going for $600 a pound in local markets."

He pulled his hair back from his face. "I left the drug-runners for the ginseng rustlers." He shot her a wry smile.

"Saving the world one energy drink at a time," she said,

her mouth tweaking up. Then her expression darkened. "How long do you think we should stay here? Can they find us?"

"I don't know—to any of it." He turned, walked over to the campfire, low and crackling. On the other side of the ring, he'd erected the small, two-person Coleman tent, unrolled the single sleeping bag. He'd probably camp out by the fire, let her curl up in the warmth. They'd shared the MRE—cold lasagna—from his pack, but he'd given her the Hershey bar. "I should have thought this through better, maybe. But I saw the skunk and the first thing I thought was—"

"My stalker had found us."

She sat down on the wooden log, held her hands to the fire.

He wished. He climbed over the log, settled beside her. "No. I thought maybe Lorenzo or his cohorts had tracked me down." He ran a hand behind his neck, kneaded the muscles there.

"Do you really think they'd leave a skunk in warning?"

She was probably right about that. "If it was the Mexican cartel, we'd probably be dead."

"That's reassuring. But you don't really think they're still looking for you, do you?"

"If someone killed my men, burned my drug supply and got away, costing me millions . . . ?" He raised a shoulder.

He let his words linger, didn't elaborate, the past feeling suddenly close enough to whisper in his ear, tickle cold fingers down his spine.

"I should probably tell you that there was someone standing in the woods watching us the other night. She took pictures."

"I know."

He glanced at her, and she met his glance, lifted a

shoulder. "Candy. Wanting your side of the story about Darrin, right? I saw the envelope in the truck."

Oh. She stared at him then, made a wry face.

And suddenly, just like that, her behavior, her sudden about-face in his life clicked into place. Like a hand reaching down to grab ahold of his heart, it squeezed with a sudden crazy hope. "You were leaving . . . to protect me?" He could barely form the words, let alone let them sink in. "Why?"

She said nothing, but reached out and poked a long birch stick into the fire. It sparked into the night, tiny fireflies crackling against the darkness.

"Kenzie?"

"Because I care about you, Luke." Soft, sharp. Almost angry. "And I don't want you to get hurt."

He drew in a breath, the hand releasing, and with it a flood of heat. "You don't need to worry about me—"

"Because you don't need anyone?" She didn't look at him, just pushed the coals into the night. "Because you think they're better off without you?"

He said nothing, looked away. The shadows grew from the forest to meet the twilight, magenta and amber, the wind rushing against the trees.

He drew a breath. "Darrin could have escaped at least twice during the three months we were held. I was . . . in no shape to travel. And he knew it. I kept telling him to go, but he refused to leave me." He closed his eyes, shook his head. "But the first chance I had, I left him."

He felt her hand on his, and he pulled away.

"Luke, you had no choice."

"I *had* a choice." He looked at her then. "I should have gone back for him. Should have dragged him out."

He got up, stalked away from the fire, feeling the heat of the flames behind him. "I can't get him out of my head, him

111

telling me to go. And me, actually leaving." He closed his eyes. "I should have stayed."

"And died with him." He felt more than heard her as Kenzie came up behind him, pressed her hand between his shoulder blades. Her voice turned low, so gentle it twisted inside him. "That's it, isn't it, Luke. You can't bear the fact that he died, and you lived, and you can't repay him. So instead of living your life, you simply refuse to live at all."

"I live—"

"Yeah, in a Silver Stream so far from civilization, I doubt they could find you on a satellite photo. You're the living, breathing definition of a hermit, and it's completely unnecessary. You're so bent on punishing yourself for your mistakes—"

"People get hurt around me!" He didn't mean for his voice to thunder, and the echo of it reverberated into the night. "Good people, like Darrin, and . . ." His voice dropped. "My father."

She stared at him, her eyes so soft they could wound. "Welcome to relationships, Luke. People who love each other occasionally hurt each other. They leave fingerprints and bruises on each other's lives, and you know why? Because when you love someone, your heart is tender toward them. Vulnerable. But that doesn't mean we should live with our dukes up, thickening our hide to people who love us. We're supposed to feel the presence of other people in our lives. You know what your sister said to me today?"

He didn't want to know. But the refusal wouldn't emerge.

"She said that she wished you'd get it through your thick head that she loves you. And that yeah, you made some mistakes, but she's never stopped believing the best in you." She pitched her voice low then and pressed her hand to his chest. "And my guess is that your father feels the same way."

He winced then. Looked away, at the final shimmer of sun on the horizon.

Shook his head.

"You only say that because it's easier to hold everyone at arm's length than it is to let them into the soft tissue of your heart."

For such a soft tone, it had lethal aim. "You don't know anything about it—"

"Oh, really? I think I do." She walked around him, her eyes sparking in the firelight. "You know the reason I keep taking Hayes 006 roles? Well I'll tell you—it's because I'm afraid, okay?"

He glanced at her, her small body radiating a fierceness that belied her words.

"I'm afraid that Hayes 006 is all I am. A fake superhero. That if I were given a chance at a real role, I'd fail. And that's not the worst of it, because every day I remember what my parents gave me, what they sacrificed for me, and I long to be more—to be this amazing actress who uses her talents to change the world. But even when I try, I fail. Maybe Greg is right—maybe I should put back on the leather bodysuit and strike a pose. Hayes 006, Bond girl wannabe."

He stared down at her, the firelight flickering against her face as the darkness enfolded him. "Kenzie—"

"I wish, for one second, that I could be the kind of person your friend Darrin was. Someone who actually does something important, or meaningful." Her expression softened. "Luke, if you had any idea how . . . how *amazing* you are? The way you play with Trevor, and how you've protected me—"

"I protected you so much we're hiding in the woods—"

"So much that you were going to give Candy that interview, weren't you?"

He drew in a breath at her aim. "I was thinking it, yeah."

"I'm a little slow, so tell me if I got this right. You were willing to break national secrets, maybe get thrown in jail, not to mention have some Mexican drug lords track you down just so the tabloids wouldn't print a picture of me—"

"And me—"

"Right and you, of course." She reached up and touched his cheek, her hand warm. "MacKenzie Grace's Secret Love Exposed."

His hand touched hers, and he found her eyes, suddenly serious. "Is that what I am? A secret love?"

Her eyes widened. She swallowed. "Secret, yeah. Love . . ." She bit her lip then, turned away, her face reddening, sliding her hand from beneath his.

But her words hung between them, in the silence of the flickering flames, in the cool breath of the night. "It's late—"

"Kenzie," he said softly, the word now filling his chest, his throat. Love. Yeah, maybe because suddenly it all became clear.

He might have been her protector, but she had the power to save him. To bring him back to the land of the living.

To furrow the soil of his heart with her words, her smile, the way she trusted him, even wanted to keep him safe. "Don't leave," he said softly, a hope more than words.

She stilled, lifted her gaze to him, question in her expression.

"Yeah, the word is love," he whispered as his hand went around her neck, as he stepped up to her. So small, so fragile, swimming in his sweatshirt, belonging to him.

He hovered just a second over her lips, meeting her eyes.

Wide, luminous, and then just at the last moment, her mouth tugged up in a smile.

And that's all it took. He covered her mouth with his, diving into that place where he knew he could unlock the dark places, unfold the creased, hard wrinkles of his heart.

Heat and joy and the exploding sense of losing himself and not caring, not wanting to yank it all back and flee.

Her mouth yielded to his, opening for his possession. She made a sweet little noise in the back of her throat and he found himself sweeping her body into his arms, hers around his neck.

Kenzie. He wasn't sure exactly what he'd done with the man he knew, the man blissfully lost as he sat down before the fire, her in his lap, running his hands through her hair, tasting the chocolate bar he'd given her and the piquant bite of coffee, smelling the scent of the fresh Cherokee forest on her skin. Her body fit perfectly into his embrace and he reluctantly pulled back and traced her face with his fingertips, staring into her eyes. His heart thundered, cumbrous in his chest.

She framed his face with her hands, her fingers brushing the prickle of his beard. A smile lit her lips. "MacKenzie Grace's Secret Love Exposed. For once, I believe the tabloids got it right."

He touched his forehead to hers. "Oh no, what have I gotten myself into? I've fallen in love with a superhero."

She laughed then, sweet and full. "And I've fallen in love with a renegade hermit. We're a pair."

Fallen. In Love.

He could barely swallow, not wanting to think past right now. Tonight. To keeping them alive and warm until he could unknot his thoughts and find a clear path to tomorrow.

If he could, he'd never leave this place.

The wind sifted through the trees, licked the flames of the campfire. She trembled, the night sounds coming to life in the shiver of the trees, the owls. "You're cold," he said quietly, drawing her close to him.

"I'll be okay."

"Such a hero." He pressed a kiss to the top of her head. "I was thinking, there's a cell tower about a half-mile from here. I can sometimes get reception if I hike to the top of the ridge. I'll do that in the morning and get ahold of Greg."

She stilled beside him. "I'm not going anywhere without you."

He closed his eyes, but the words soaked in, filled him. *We'll see.* "Okay."

She tucked herself in. "If you promise to behave yourself, I will let you share your sleeping bag."

He made a face, lifted his head. "It's yours, Kenzie. I was going to sleep out here by the fire."

She looked up at him. "Not on your life. Listen, I have lethal karate skills. I'll keep you in line."

"Indeed." He studied her face for a moment, then smiled. He picked her up and carried her into the tent. "Really, I promise to be a good boy."

She crawled in and unzipped the bag, climbing in fully clothed. She flung it over him, but the narrow bag only slid off his shoulders.

"It's a mummy bag," he said. "I didn't consider fugitives when I bought it." He leaned back, pulling her against him, tucking her in the bag, close. Her hand settled on his chest. He kissed her hair. "I wasn't going to sleep anyway. I have to figure out how to get us out of this mess."

"Us," she said, a soft hum in her voice. "And, cut."

Kenzie laced her fingers into Luke's grip, his hand knotted in hers. Despite the chill that descended with the night, she had stopped shivering when Luke turned her on her side, then folded his body to nestle against hers, his presence warm against her, even through the sleeping bag. She'd given him back his sweatshirt, but couldn't help but think he might be cold, sleeping on the hard ground without a blanket. But he seemed warmer than she, his knees tucked in behind her as she lay with her head in the nook of his arm, facing away from him.

Trying not to think about tomorrow.

"Maybe we can just stay here," she said quietly, into the husk of night.

"It would certainly make things easier," Luke said quietly. His warm breath caressed her neck, the wild allure of the woods and night scenting his skin. It was like curling up next to a mountain lion, calm on the outside, but under the surface, the coiled sense of listening to every rustle of the trees, gauging the night for danger, ready to pounce. "But first, I need to figure out who is after us."

She ran her fingers into the ruff of hair on his sinewy arms. "I mean, here, in Tennessee."

He fell quiet then, his breath drawing in and out.

"I don't want to leave."

"I don't want you to leave, either." Simple words, roughened along the edges and she knew how it cost him to say it.

She rolled onto her back and met his eyes in the wax of moonlight through the mesh window, the silvery glow on his face lighting the cedar in his whiskers. She ran her thumb against the shag. "What if I stayed?"

His mouth tugged up, a rueful smile. Then he leaned down and kissed her, such an aching softness in his touch she couldn't help but wonder if he might be saying good-bye. He sighed and rolled onto his back, pulling her against his chest, twining his fingers through her hair. "You have a life in Hollywood."

"What if I don't want that life anymore?"

Silence.

She hoisted herself up on one elbow, and he looked at her. "Today, at the picnic, I felt more like myself than I have in years. I watched your sister and her husband play with Trevor and realized—this is the life I want."

She leaned down again, staring at the amber glow of the tent. "I had a simple life as a child. We didn't have much—I lived in a trailer on land my parents were given by my grandfather. We walked to church on Sundays—walked everywhere, really, and my dad, even though he was mentally challenged, loved to work in his garden. And it was impressive. I remember walking through his tomato plants, taller than I was, and cucumbers and strawberries and even a pumpkin patch. My mother canned it all. Then in the wintertime, every Sunday evening, my mother would open a jar of pickles and Daddy and I would turn on the television and we'd watch *America's Funniest Home Videos*. We'd laugh and vote and slurp up the pickle juice, and for some reason, it made me feel safe. Normal. As if that was the perfect life."

"It sounds like it."

"Maybe. What I didn't know was that they barely kept social services from taking me away. My parents weren't stupid—just simple. But it wasn't until I got into middle school that it started to bother me."

She closed her eyes. "I want more than anything to go back to those days when I thought my daddy was the most heroic, amazing person in the world."

Luke fell silent beside her, but she felt his hand move down, catch hers, weaving her fingers again into his.

She sighed. "My dad got laid off from the rayon plant when I was twelve. He couldn't get a job for months, yet he refused to go on food stamps. Then, one day I saw him after school pushing a wide broom down the hallway and I realized he'd become the school janitor." She closed her eyes against the memory, the swell of regret.

"I was mortified," she said softly. "Then he started to get ribbing from the football players and other jocks about picking up their towels and cleaning out their lockers for them. He doesn't have strong verbal skills, and sometimes has a hard time forming his thoughts out loud. They would finish his sentences and mock him."

She felt Luke tense, a reflex that suggested protection, and she loved him even more for it.

Except, "The worst part is that I felt ashamed of them too." She drew in a breath and Luke shifted, leaning up to look at her. She couldn't meet his eyes.

"I longed to run away, to pretend I came from a rich, beautiful, smart family. I became a master at pretending I was someone else. Some normal person from one of those families I saw on the Funniest Home Videos. Probably that was why I landed every major role in the school plays in high school. But I knew I needed to leave Harmony, so I put everything I had into school, got straight As, and landed a partial scholarship to Duke. I drove myself to college and didn't look back. I got involved in theater and started landing more roles. Then on one opening night, I looked into the audience and saw my parents. They were sitting in the second row, wearing their Sunday best . . . and . . ."

She pressed a hand to her mouth, her voice trembling. Luke brushed her hair from her face, said nothing.

Finally, "My mother was crying. I thought it was because she was so moved by my performance, but . . . it was a sort of a risqué play called, *Move Over, Mrs. Markham*. It had a lot of sexual innuendos, and while it's a hilarious comedy, I'm not sure they understood it. They just saw their daughter hopping in and out of the arms of the men on stage and . . . they were upset."

He hadn't moved a muscle, hadn't twitched at her story, but one eyebrow drew down.

"I was suddenly mortified. And the worst part was, after the show, I didn't go out to meet them. I knew they'd driven three hours to see me, maybe even taken the bus, and instead of going out to meet them, I snuck out through the back entrance."

"Because you were embarrassed?"

"No. That's the worst part." She ran her fingertips against the moisture in her eyes, reclaiming her voice. "I was more embarrassed that they had made a scene than for anything I'd done. It was just a play—but they acted as if I'd sold my soul. And . . ." She shook her head, and her eyes flooded again, a trail sliding down her cheek. Her voice dropped. "In that moment, I wished that they weren't in my life."

She swallowed, a ball of heat in her throat. "I've never even invited them to Hollywood. Not once. And I keep saying it's because they wouldn't understand, but it's because I am ashamed. Of them. Of me. Of the fact they worked so hard to get me through college—they paid for everything the scholarship didn't cover—and I've done nothing with it. Sure, I've made money, but I can't help but think they expected great things from me, and I've let them down. And they're right. I'm a Christian, and yet there's nothing of my faith that shows up in my life."

She looked at him, then, undone by the concern in his eyes, the sweet warmth of his expression. "Sometimes I just wish I could go back and just be that little girl eating pickles."

He traced her face with his fingers. "And that's what you were today?"

She nodded.

"Weren't you voted one of America's most beautiful women?"

"You did Google me!"

He grinned. Winked. Pressed a kiss to her mouth.

She closed her eyes, wanting to sink into his embrace, but he pulled away and something in his eyes turned serious. "I'm not sure you were meant to just eat pickles."

She frowned.

"My father always said that it wasn't about what you do for God, but whether you belong to God that matters. We spend a lot of time trying to make sense out of our lives by striving to do amazing things. But, according to my father, you can't *do* Christianity. You must be . . . the *doing* comes out of the *being*."

Something flickered in his eyes, a memory, maybe, because he suddenly lay back, his hands on his chest. "I'd forgotten he said that. But I can hear his voice in my head."

He gave a low chuckle as Pop's words ran through his mind. "'Luke, don't forget, "I have been crucified with Christ and I no longer live, but Christ lives in me. The life I now live in the body, I live by faith in the Son of God, who loves me and gave his life for me."' I can still hear him, helping me with my memorization. We always had to memorize in King James." He looked over at her. "I've been trying all my life to figure out that verse. But I think . . . I think it's about bacon."

"Bacon?"

"My dad said the difference between contribution and commitment can be found in a plate of bacon and eggs."

"Come again?"

"The chicken made a contribution. But the pig went all in. We are not called to make a contribution. We are called to make a commitment. So, if our hearts are right, then our actions follow."

"I guess it's a matter of where our hearts belong," she said quietly.

He slipped his hand again in hers as the night moved around them in wind and forest noises.

And that was the problem, wasn't it?

Maybe she simply wouldn't think beyond tonight and tucking herself back into the curve of Luke's embrace, close her eyes against the dark, masculine smell of him, as he folded his arm over her. Pattern her breath to his as she reached for that place of safety, of peace.

Right where she longed to remain.

She woke to the sounds of the morning—sparrows and chickadees calling from the trees, the patter of dew as it shook off the trees onto the tent. And a chill running down her back.

Luke was gone.

She sat up, unzipped the door, and stared out into the campfire area. No warm coals, no fire beckoned with a pot of coffee on the grate. She untangled herself from the sleeping bag and climbed out, pulling on her shoes. "Luke?"

The bear pack still hung from the tree where he'd hoisted it last night, but fresh kindling lay by the fire pit. Maybe he was out gathering firewood.

A low mist clung to the valley below, cotton that lay over the tumble of rocks and forest. In the distance golden sunlight gilded the mountains, tipping them with rose-gold.

Luke's words from last night found her, tiptoeing into her mind. *So, if our hearts are right, then our actions follow.*

Kenzie wandered over to stand at the edge of the cliff. Maybe that was the point. She couldn't remember the last time she felt her heart settled in the right place. But here, right now, she could taste it, the peace.

The air was warming, the sun burning away the low hanging haze—the makings of a glorious morning.

She *could* belong to Luke's world—more than anything, it felt like home. What if she said good-bye, forever, to Hayes O'Brien's 006 world and started over?

She curled her arms around her waist, hollow with hunger, a shiver rushing through her.

Yes. She'd stay here with Luke. Build the life she really wanted.

Footsteps sounded behind her and she turned to see Luke crossing toward her. He still wore the sweatshirt, his dark blond hair tousled with the night's sleep, a scruff along his chin.

His expression, however, belied trouble. "We gotta go," he said as he headed toward the tent, pulling out the sleeping bag.

Huh? She watched as he stuffed the bag into a sack. "Where were you?"

He walked over to the bear pack hanging from the tree and cut it down. "I hiked up to the ridge to see if I could get cell reception."

The pack fell into his strong arms. He strapped the sleeping bag to the pack then lifted the tent from its moorings. "I couldn't call anyone, but I had enough bars to get a text."

With a couple quick shakes, the tent collapsed. He had it rolled into its stuff sack in moments. "They caught your stalker, and Greg's on his way to Tennessee to get you."

"What—who was it?"

He clipped the tent bag onto his pack then cinched it up tight, grabbing the water bottle still sitting out by the fire pit. Slinging the bag over his shoulders, he stood up. "Greg didn't say."

He held out his hand. "It's over. It's time to go, MacKenzie Grace."

She'd never seen her life dismantled so quickly.

Chapter Ten

"What if I don't want to go back to LA?"

Kenzie sat on the truck bench, her hand braced on the overhead loop by the door, turned slightly in her seat so as to sear him with her gaze. "You have this little issue of forgetting you're not the boss of me."

"There's where you're wrong," Luke said, jerking the truck around the ruts in the dirt road. "Until you're on a plane and safely away from here . . ." He swallowed, corrected. "Away from *me*, then yeah, I'm the boss of you. Which I sort of forgot back there. But it became crystal clear the minute I got Greg's text."

Actually, it became crystal clear last night when she suggested that she throw away everything she'd worked for to camp out with him in the woods. He'd managed to keep his heart from thundering, his breath even, but no way, no how, would he let her sacrifice her amazing career for . . . well, him. Besides, after today, he wouldn't have a future to share with her.

He softened his voice. "Kenzie, it's over. You're safe—

Greg told me they found your attacker. I know it's been . . . trying, but you can go back to your real life now."

"Trying?" She sucked in a breath as if he'd hit her. "It hasn't been trying, Luke. It's been . . . it's been magnificent. Amazing. And . . . *what happened*? Last night I told you that I wanted this, I wanted us, and I thought you did too—"

"I did. I do—" The words slipped out before he could arrest them. He tightened his hold on the steering wheel with whitened fists.

"Then why don't you want me?"

He winced, tapped his brakes as they finally emerged from the forest onto the main dirt road. He stared ahead, managing to keep his hands on the steering wheel before he did something stupid like reach out for her. But his voice betrayed him. "I want you more than you know, Kenzie. You . . . you made me believe that someone could still love me—"

"I do love you Luke—"

And now he shook his head. "You can't love me. It's no good. Because I've decided to tell Darrin's wife the truth. All of it."

Only the beating of his heart fell between them.

"But her book—"

"Yeah. She'll probably tell the world, and yeah, that means I'll probably be brought up on charges of treason. But I couldn't sleep last night, thinking about . . . well, the fact that I can't live with myself anymore. My heart screaming to do one thing while my actions do another."

He shook his head. "I don't care about Lorenzo tracking me down, finishing me off. Sure, I want to live, but I'm not afraid. And I'm not afraid of going to jail either." He turned to her, his voice quiet and tight despite the roar building in his chest. "I'm afraid of living every day with this darkness inside, unable to forgive myself."

He tightened his jaw against the sudden rush of tears to

her eyes, the compassion in her expression. He couldn't bear it and looked away. "I am ashamed of myself. And *that* is what I can't live with."

"Luke, you have nothing to be ashamed about."

"I do! Don't you see, Kenzie? I chose to save my life instead of saving my brother's life and for that I cannot ever be forgiven. It's as if I killed him. But what's worse, is I kill him every day over and over again with my silence. It would have been better had I died, and he lived."

"Greater love hath no man than he lay down his life for his friend," Kenzie said softly.

He shook his head. "I did not lay my life down for my friend. He laid it down for me."

"But isn't that the point of the gospel? God laid His life down for us to save us because He loved us. So that we can then go and love others. Darrin gave his life for you, yes, but not so you could spend your life in shame, punishing yourself. The way forward is love, Luke. Not punishment and the burnt offering of your life. You've been given life so you can use it to love others. People like your sister, and Trevor. People like . . . me."

He looked at her, and oh, he wanted her to stay. Could feel the words welling up inside him, the longing for it, the way she could, with a word, silence the demons inside, untangle his confusion.

Make him feel.

He gave her the hint of a smile, reached out and touched her hair. He couldn't remember the last time he held a woman in his arms, and last night, with her tucked in beside him, him doing his best to behave himself—yeah she'd seeded all his forbidden dreams of waking up beside her every single day for the rest of his life.

"Please don't make me leave you," Kenzie said softly.

And he couldn't argue with her. Not when he wanted her

words with every breath in his body. He managed a tight nod and she scooted over next to him on the seat, like they might be in high school.

He put his arm around her as he turned onto the dirt road, winding back to his cabin, sorting through scenarios, trying to find one that didn't end up with him in Leavenworth.

He slowed as they crossed the bridge, and he caught the flash of red through the trees. A car—it took another glimpse of it to recognize his sister's Ford Escape. He tapped the brakes, his heart thick in his chest.

"What's the matter? You're white," Kenzie said, looking up at him.

"My sister has visited me a sum total of three times—and all three were bad news." He pulled up behind her car. The cabin appeared dark, however, no sign of his sister.

The skunk still hung, hard and decaying from his door.

He paused, a knife tickling down his spine. If Ruthann saw the skunk and didn't turn right around to find Cooper then . . . "Maybe . . . just wait here?"

"Luke—"

"For once, Kenzie, please stay put. Something doesn't feel right."

Next to him, she bristled, but she backed away, sat with her arms crossed by the door. He turned to her, his gaze tracking over her face. "You're so beautiful when you're mad," he said and kissed her, fast and hard.

Then he opened his glove compartment and pulled out his Beretta.

Her mouth opened, but he slid out of the car before she had a chance to respond.

Luke left the door open, approaching the house.

"Ruthie? Are you here?" He stopped at her car, found it empty, her purse in the passenger seat. A cup of coffee was stashed between the seats in front and a McDonald's cup wilted in the cup holder in the backseat, the straw half-chewed.

No child in the safety seat.

Luke stiffened, holding the gun down, not wanting to scare his nephew should he come bounding out of the house.

The door eased open, and his sister came out. "Luke!"

The claws in his chest eased. "Ruth—" But his breath caught when he saw her expression. Pale, shaking.

And right behind her, Trevor, being pushed out of the door, the barrel of a 9mm, not unlike Luke's own, jammed against his little blond head.

Luke went cold, his body stiffening as Patsy Gerard stepped out onto the porch. He remembered Darrin's wife—widow—as petite, blonde, sweet as the day was long. This version had greasy, dirty blonde hair, and had put on enough weight to suggest stress. "Hey, Luke. Took you long enough. Ruth called you two hours ago."

She had? But he didn't mention the fact her call hadn't come in.

He kept his voice low, trying to reach for calm, untangle the situation. "Did you leave the skunk?"

She glanced at the door. "No, actually. It seems we'll be forming a line."

Patsy motioned for Ruth to get on her knees. Moved the gun from Trevor's head to Ruthann's and with the motion, a hand reached through Luke, tightened around his throat.

"I just came to talk, Luke." Patsy's voice shook, not a great indicator of her mental state. "But it's gotten complicated."

"Let them go, Patsy. I came to talk too. Really."

"Then drop your gun!" Her voice shrilled, high, panicked, and this was exactly how someone got shot, even accidentally.

He swallowed the dark fist of panic and dropped the gun

into the soft earth. He raised his hands, his voice steady. "Please, Patsy. Darrin wouldn't want this. Let them walk out here, to me."

She moved the gun back to Trevor's head, and he whimpered. The sound if it could gut Luke, tear him in half.

"Please, Patsy." And shoot, now *his* voice shook.

Brave Trevor stood, tears running down his cheeks.

"This is how it feels to be helpless, Luke." Patsy was crying too, her voice wretched. "To know that you can't save the people you love. But it's even worse when you don't know what's happening. Imagine if you were out here, alone, and all you heard was screaming. Over and over and over, but not knowing what's happening, letting your imagination have its way."

Tears cut down her cheeks. "That's my life, for the past seven years. Waking up every night, his imagined screams in my ears. Knowing I can't save him—that you *didn't* save him. And yet, guessing. Always guessing, and wishing I could understand."

"Let Trevor and Ruthann go and you won't have to guess anymore. I'll tell you everything—"

"I think you need to know how that feels, Luke." She clamped Trevor around the neck. "Then, maybe you'll understand—"

"I understand, Patsy! Because you might imagine his screams, but guess what—I hear them!"

She flinched, but he didn't care. He cut his voice back, took a step toward her.

"Only, they aren't screams. They're Darrin yelling at me to run. To leave. To live." He thumped his chest. "That's what I have to live with every single day. The knowledge that he gave his life for mine. Even knowing how much he wanted to come back to you."

Her mouth tightened.

He took another step forward, and Trevor let out a cry.

"Fine. Okay, listen. You know we were taken, right? And it doesn't matter so much why we were there as what happened when we got there. Darrin wasn't hurt when we were taken—not much, anyway, but I was. I busted up my knee enough to make escape impossible. Darrin kept me alive. He set my leg, he gave me his food, he arranged the escape with the SEALs. And when the time came, he pushed me into the arms of my rescuers and took a bullet—a few bullets—for me. Then, as they dragged me away, he stayed behind and pulled the pin on the grenade that affected our escape."

He said it as quickly as he could, hoping not to land in the memories, the smell of fire as the camp exploded, the SEALs shouting at him, the feel of his buddy's blood on his hands.

The look on Darrin's face as he roared at him to run.

Not afraid. Determined. Even, peaceful.

And that's what he'd forgotten. Darrin, wanting to sacrifice for him. Being the friend Luke longed to be—would have been had the op gone south and he'd been the one bleeding to death.

He wouldn't have begrudged Patsy and Darrin one second of happiness, of a life together.

The way forward is love, Luke.

"Darrin loved you, Patsy." He put everything he had into his voice. "Every day he'd talk about you, how you met, how beautiful you were, the funny, quirky things he missed about you. I thought it was to keep me from focusing on the pain, but I think it was a reminder, for him, of the joy he'd had, and still had, waiting for him. I think he was trying to keep himself alive."

Patsy was shaking now. "He should have come home to me."

Luke nodded. But, "Please don't shoot my family, Patsy. That's not what Darrin would want."

Her eyes glistened, her jaw tight. Then, "No. You're right. But it's what I want."

"Patsy!"

And then time slowed as Ruthann screamed and Trevor wrestled against Patsy's grip.

The gun went off just as Pasty jerked, hard, flew off the porch in a tangle of limbs and screams, tackled from behind.

Whoever took Patsy off the front porch, landed hard on top of her in the dirt.

Kenzie. The realization clicked a second before Luke launched himself at them.

Patsy elbowed her assailant in the face, and somewhere in the mass of bodies, the gun—

A shot ripped through the air.

It stopped Luke cold.

Kenzie jerked back, fell off Patsy, wide-eyed, her hands on her stomach, her mouth open.

Blood spilled into the loamy soil.

"Kenzie!"

"Kenzie, please, please don't die on me."

Luke's voice reached into the darkness and yanked her, fast, with an agonizing scream from the fingers that wanted to pull her under. She blinked against a strobe of too many sensations—light falling through the trees, a consuming fire in her gut, a metallic taste in her mouth. "What—"

"You were shot, baby. Just, hang on." Luke leaned into her vision, sweat beading on his temples. "The gun went off under Pasty—the bullet went through Patsy and landed in you. Don't move." He looked up away from her, yelling at someone. "Hurry up!"

"I'm right here." And then Ruthann appeared, shoved a wad of towels and sheets into Luke's arms. "Stanch the bleeding as best you can." She pressed two fingers along Kenzie's neck, finding her pulse. "A little fast, but maybe we can keep her from going into shock long enough to get to the hospital."

"This is going to hurt, I'm sorry." Luke pressed the towel over the burn in her abdomen. She closed her eyes, bit back a scream. But Luke was right there, his sweaty forehead on hers, his eyes taking in her pain. "We gotta pack it so we can move you." He took a sheet and ripped it down the middle, his hands bloody, shaking. Then he hurt her again as he lifted her and slid the sheet under her.

"I'm sorry," he said again, over and over.

He tied the sheet down tight as Ruthann attended Patsy. Kenzie turned her head, saw Patsy's pale, drawn face, eyes closed. "Is she dead?"

"Not yet," Ruthann said and glanced at Luke. "Her chest is filling up—I think the bullet went through one of her lungs. We need some towels over here!"

He moved to Patsy, repeated the procedure on the gaping hole in her chest.

Ruthann took off for the house again, and Kenzie's eyes followed her, spied Trevor, unhurt and standing just a few feet away on the porch. She gave him a little smile. "It'll be okay, Trevor."

His eyes simply widened.

"It's not going to be okay!" Luke had returned to her, his blue eyes thick with emotion. "What were you thinking, Kenz?" He leaned back, his hands shaking now as he stared down at her.

"I was thinking that I didn't want the man I loved to die in front of me," she said quietly.

He let out a breath and closed his eyes. Then, abruptly, he leaned forward and pressed a hard kiss on her forehead. "I'm not going to let you die."

"You'd better not. I'm a big movie star."

"You're a big troublemaker," Luke said, but she got the smallest of smiles.

Ruthann returned with blankets. "We'll get there faster if we drive them to the hospital."

"Agreed. Spread it out. We'll roll her up in one. Put her in the back of the truck."

"Please don't let him drive," Kenzie said feebly, then groaned as Luke lifted her into the blanket.

He tucked it around her. "Stop talking."

He did the same to Patsy, carrying her to the truck.

"I'll ride in back," Ruthann said.

Luke appeared again, scooping Kenzie into his arms. He met her eyes as he spoke to Ruthann. "No, you drive."

He tucked her into his chest as he carried her to the bed of the truck, climbed in with her.

Ruthann must have grabbed Trevor and buckled him in because moments later, they were turning around, the treetops moving overhead.

She sucked in a breath as they jostled hard down the dirt road, Luke's arms tightening around her.

"Luke—"

"Yeah, baby." His face was white as he offered her a grim smile.

"This isn't your fault.'

A muscle twitched on his face, and she knew she'd hit the mark.

"You're not Hayes O'Brien," he said quietly. "You shouldn't have risked your life for me."

133

"You don't get to call all the shots, Ranger Rick. Maybe I didn't want to lose you. Maybe I want to grow old with you, and that doesn't include watching you die in your front yard."

"I'm supposed to protect you!"

"Maybe we're supposed to protect each other," she said. "I love you, Luke. And I sat there, listening to you pour out the story to Patsy, and I realized that I needed to let love lead the way too. I've always let my goals, what I thought were my dreams be in charge—leaving home, the Hollywood lights. But maybe there's a better way. Maybe I can give my heart to God, and he can figure this out. Maybe I don't have to be always trying so hard—I can just be. And that's when I realized . . . I might not be Hayes O'Brien, but I do have some of her moves."

She cried out as they went over another pothole.

"Drive better!" Luke shouted and banged on the cab in front of him.

"Do you want to get there or not?" Ruthann shouted back through the opening.

Focusing back on Kenzie, he cupped his hand on her face. "What are you talking about?"

She groaned, her entire body burning. "There's a scene, just like this, in *Spy Under Fire*, where Hayes has to sneak in through a back entrance, and tackle the bad guy—or gal, rather. So I remembered the window in the back, and how I opened it when we had the fire in the house, and I snuck out of the truck and went around the back and there it was, still open. I waited until she moved the gun away from Trevor, and then—well, in the movie, no one got shot."

"This isn't the movies."

She closed her eyes. "Bummer. Because in the movies, this is where the hero declares his undying love—"

"I love you, Kenzie. Dying and undying and shoot,

Ruthann drive faster!" He lifted his hand from where he held it over her towels. It came away red. "Just live through this, and we'll talk about you pretending you're a superhero."

"I am a superhero," she said softly.

He kissed her. Sweetly, as if to shut her up, but enough for her to know he believed it too.

When he lifted his head his eyes glistened, and he looked away.

They hit the highway, and Luke pulled out his cell phone, thumbed open a contact, and put it to his ear. She closed her eyes.

"Are you here yet?" His voice, dark, short.

A pause then, "Meet me at the hospital—Kenzie's hurt."

Deep breath. "Take a breath, dude!" His voice turned into a shout. "I know, sheesh. Just be there."

He hung up.

She opened her eyes.

"Your bossy agent," he said.

"Runs in the family."

He didn't smile, his expression grim as he looked away from her, watching the road. "Just wait until the press gets ahold of this."

And, she knew then, that if she didn't do something after he deposited her into Greg's keeping, he'd walk away. Because with his words, she saw her world crashing over them. *MacKenzie Grace, Movie Star, Injured in Backwoods Shootout.*

He was right. The press would dig away at her, at Patsy and the past until they unearthed it all, Luke reliving that day over and over, digging a hole right through him.

Greg would put her on the first plane to LA, to resume her life.

She reached up, put her hand around his lapel. "Call Candy."

135

He stared down at her, frowning. "What?"

"Call Candy. I have something to tell her."

"No."

Stubborn, frustrating . . . but she knew how to deal with leading men who thought they were the stars. She softened her voice, added a tremor.

"Please, trust me?"

"Greg is going to kill you. Or me. Or both of us." But he got out his phone. "What do you want me to tell her?"

"To meet me at the hospital for the scoop of a lifetime."

Chapter Eleven

Luke was on his feet nearly before his sister finished braking in front of the Normandy ER. No more than a medical center, it served as the stopping place to triage the wounded before sending serious patients to nearby Johnson City for more extensive trauma care.

He had no doubt that Kenzie would be on her way, maybe even life-flighted the bullet still tearing through her body to cause damage.

As if to confirm his dread, she moaned as he lifted her out of the back end, settled her on a gurney. Two more attendants come to retrieve Patsy, but Luke refused to release his grip on Kenzie's hand as they wheeled her under the bright lights into the hallway.

"Wait!" Kenzie said. Pale, her skin nearly translucent in the florescence, she appeared battered and as close to death as anyone he'd ever seen. She reached up and grabbed Luke's shirt. "Candy—is she here yet?"

He frowned at her. "Who cares—"

"Find her, Luke."

"I'm right here, honey." The voice turned him, and Luke

bit back an urge to wrap his hands around the reporter's throat.

"Good," Kenzie said, her breath weak. "Because this is all you get." Then she tugged Luke's shirt, pulling him down. She wrapped a hand around his neck and then, with more strength than he thought she possessed, she kissed him.

Not a sweet kiss, either, but something of possession, of ownership. Of decision.

And she held him long enough for Candy to get the money shot.

But he didn't care—not when he could pour into her everything he wanted to say. Needed to say.

Including good-bye. Because once she lived through this . . .

She let him go, her hand dropping away. "My secret love in the woods."

Her secret love . . . and then he got it.

Take that, Candy. No more blackmail.

As if he cared. But maybe—yes, there she went, protecting him again. Deflecting the media.

The attendants parked her in the ER bay. "Do not let her die," Luke growled to the doctor.

"Maybe you should step outside, sir." This from a well-meaning nurse who clearly knew nothing about him, or the fact that they'd have to wrestled him out of here if they planned on dislodging him from Kenzie's side.

Kenzie opened her eyes and, as if to confirm his thoughts, "Luke, don't go."

"See?" he hissed at the nurse.

A nurse strapped an oxygen mask over Kenzie's face. Another nurse was starting an IV. A man in scrubs looked up at Luke. "What's her name?"

"MacKenzie. MacKenzie Grace."

A flicker of recognition, another of shock, then the nurse bent to insert the line.

The doctor rolled back the sodden blanket, and Luke braced himself against the blood, so much of it, saturating the towel, his wrapping. The doctor peeled the wrapping back and Kenzie made a noise.

"Easy."

"Sir—"

Luke raised his hand in surrender.

"Step back, sir—" This from the nurse. "We need room to work."

He stiffened, then a hand tightened on his arm. "Luke. C'mon, dude."

Greg. He stood in his jeans and a T-shirt under a suit coat, looking grim. His red-rimmed eyes evidenced the overnight flight from LA. "Take a breath. Let them work on her." He urged Luke from Kenzie's bedside.

Luke stepped back, breathing hard, wincing at the gaping wound in her abdomen. Had to have hit a kidney . . .

Greg led him over to a chair, eased him into it. Then he walked over to the sink, grabbed a washcloth, wet it.

He returned, put the washcloth in Luke's hands. "You're a mess. Your face is covered in blood, not to mention your hands and your shirt. Let's get you cleaned up."

"I'm not leaving her!"

"No one said you were. Sheesh. I'll get you some scrubs."

He left Luke to wipe his face, wincing when he saw the blood streaked into the washcloth. He worked the red from the cracks in his hand.

They'd put Kenzie on a heart monitor, oxygen.

Greg returned with towels and a set of scrubs. "Courtesy the Normandy Hospital. I found you a shower."

"Later."

Greg set the bundle on the counter then turned to watch

them work on Kenzie. Luke stood beside him, feeling lightheaded as he watched the heart monitor, as they sedated her, as the oxygen rose and fell to help her breathe.

"What happened?" Greg finally said quietly.

"It's my fault," Luke said. "Patsy Gerard, the wife of a buddy who died in Mexico, finally decided she needed to know the truth." He gestured to the team working on Patsy in the other ER bay.

"She showed up at my house, and what I can piece together is that my sister came looking for me and Patsy took her and my nephew hostage. Kenzie got the drop on her when Patsy lifted her gun to shoot me. They fell together, and I think the gun must have gone off."

"So this Patsy wasn't out for truth as much as she was revenge."

He hadn't thought about it that way, but . . . he lifted a shoulder in a shrug. "I guess so."

Greg sighed. "Kenzie's always fancied herself as a superhero. Always wanted to save the world." Luke looked at him. Greg appeared drawn, as if he had real feelings for Kenzie that might have gone beyond the agent-client relationship. Then he scrubbed a hand through his hair and glanced at Luke. "We found the stalker. It was her ex's girlfriend. She was jealous of Kenzie."

The heart monitor started to beep, and Luke startled. He felt Greg's hand on his arm, didn't even realize he had moved forward, like he could actually do something. Anything.

And then, as he stood there, watching, the monitor flatlined.

"Oh . . ." Luke's knees started to buckle, his head light, spinning, and Greg grabbed him around the waist.

"Kenzie!"

Greg muscled him out of the room as the attendants grabbed the paddles, got him as far as the hall before Luke rounded on him. He took a swing, which Greg ducked, grabbing his lapel and shoving him up against the wall.

"I know I can't hold you here for long, but breathe, Luke. They'll get her back—just breathe. And don't go in there."

He let him go and Luke leaned over, gripping his knees, his world spinning as monitors blared in the ER. Behind Greg, the door closed.

Luke slid to the floor. "She can't die." He sunk his head into his hands. "Please . . . don't let her die."

Greg sat next to him. "If I could keep her alive by sheer will, I would—

"No, not you." Luke got up, stalked down the hall. Stood for a long moment, staring at the ER.

Then he took off in a quick walk down the hallway, turning through the double doors and striding outside, into the cool breath of the late afternoon.

The smell of sunshine in the warm air slid over him. He stalked across the parking lot and through the doors of the resident care center.

Missy saw him coming. "Did Ruthann find you?"

He frowned, but didn't slow. "Why?"

"You father was lucid. He woke up this morning saying your name." She followed him down the hall. "But I don't know if he's—"

He rounded on her, not caring that his eyes burned, his chest rising and falling, so near to tears it scared him. "I don't care if he knows me. *I* know *him*, and right now, I need him."

He pushed into his father's room.

The old preacher lay in the bed, eyes closed. Sleeping, probably, and Luke didn't want to wake him. He liked to think that, deep down, under the layers of confusion, his father somehow still knew him.

He sank into a chair next to the bed. Wanted to take the old man's hand, but instead simply put his head down on the soft flannel of the blanket. "Pop, she's dying and I don't know what to do. I just can't stand here and do nothing. But I don't know what to do."

I don't know what to do.

He closed his eyes.

Then, suddenly, he felt it—the hand on his head, warming him. And a voice, soft but firm, the voice he'd grown up hearing from the pulpit and beside his bed at night. "Lord, I beseech thee for my son, Luke, that you would meet his needs and grant him the peace of your presence. Help him to know that he is not alone, and that he need not be afraid anymore."

Luke looked up. His father's eyes were still closed, no evidence that he'd been speaking. His hand had slid off Luke's head, and now Luke gathered it up between his.

"Pop."

But his eyes remained closed. Still, the hand in his tightened, as if . . . as if perhaps his father had reached out beyond his dreams, caught in that place of memory, to find Luke in the present.

To remind him he wasn't alone. Luke blinked, his cheeks wet. He closed his eyes, and the words welled up inside him, probably building for so long he couldn't remember their origin, but bubbling out now.

"Oh God, I'm sorry. I'm sorry I've been so stubborn, and angry and determined to go it alone. I'm sorry I said I didn't need you, because I do. Because . . . I'm afraid. I'm so afraid, God. Of losing you. Kenzie. And my dad. And . . . myself. I want to be more, God. But I don't know how." He drew in a breath. "Please forgive me. Please heal me. Please help me to belong again to you."

The hand in his grip tightened, then. He drew a tremulous breath and looked up.

His father's blue eyes gazed on him, a smile latching on to his face. "Luke, my son. When did you get here?"

Luke found his voice out of the gravel of his chest. "Just now, Pop. Just now."

She knew she would live because she hurt everywhere. Kenzie opened her eyes to the sunlight pouring into the window, cascading over the bedsheets, across a potpourri of floral arrangements that crowded a side table.

And seated beside the bed, Luke, one hand holding up his head as he slept.

He wore more than a day's growth in his beard. He'd showered, however, the blood gone from his face, his hands, and had changed into a pair of jeans and a plain white T-shirt, his feet in flip-flops.

He looked like a surfer, and not at all the fierce soldier she'd seen negotiating for the life of his sister and nephew. Gone also was the belligerent, hermit park ranger from the woods.

Instead, a man who'd camped out beside her bed, as if contented to stay right here.

The door opened, and she looked over to see Greg tiptoe inside. He had the family jaw, the wide shoulders. But that's where the resemblance ended. Neatly coiffed, shaven, and smelling fragranced, Greg wore a sports coat, button-down shirt, and a pair of dark jeans.

"Hey there Sleeping Beauty," he said, coming over to give her a kiss on the forehead.

She put a finger to her lips and pointed at Luke. "That's the sleeping beauty," she whispered.

Greg's mouth lifted in a grin. "Poor man hasn't left your side since you came out of surgery yesterday evening." He took her hand. "You gave us a scare. Lost a lot of blood, but thankfully, they were able to get you back up and running. You'll have a scar, but I contacted a plastic surgeon who said he'll see you when you get back to LA. You'll be in in Hayes 006 form in no time."

She took a breath. "And if I don't want to be Hayes 006 anymore?"

Greg's smile widened. "Then I have a slew of other offers for you. Because ever since Nil's girlfriend—or ex-girlfriend —was arrested for blowing up your beautiful Malibu house, you've become the darling of LA. Apparently, the world loves an underdog."

She took his hand. "And if I don't want to go back to Hollywood?"

Greg's smile fell.

"Don't panic, cuz, because she's going back to LA." This from Luke, who had roused. He looked at her, traced her face with his hand, then leaned up and pressed a soft kiss to her mouth. Sweet, and over too soon. "That's where she belongs."

"No, Luke, I belong—"

"With me?"

She managed a nod, hating how her face must have betrayed the question there.

"What if I went to LA with you?"

Her eyes widened. "Really?"

"Well, I'm apparently MacKenzie Gracie's hot romance, the one she escaped LA for. I figure we need to make it a little more permanent."

"It worked." She looked at Greg, her own brilliance swelling inside her. "Candy printed it."

"Oh, she printed it all right," Greg said. "And more. The kiss—a few of them, one on a picnic table, along with a full-out expose on some karaoke night, a picnic in civil war costumes, and a crazy story about poachers who tried to have you killed."

"Poachers?"

"Cooper caught the ginseng poachers we've been tracking. Apparently, they were still covered with the stink of the skunk on their skin."

"Not Mexican drug lords, then," she said.

"Mexican warlords?" This, from Greg. "What am I missing?"

"Actually, nothing. I contacted my commander to brief him on what happened with Patsy, and he told me that the camp was completely destroyed. They've just finished tracking down the last of the leaders."

"Just in time for Patsy's book," Kenzie said.

"I read it. It's close, but not quite accurate."

"So, if we made it into a movie, then you're not in trouble?"

"What are you talking about?" Greg said.

"My next docudrama. The story of unsung heroes fighting under the cover of darkness. Fiction, but we'll use enough truth to honor those who deserve it." She glanced at Luke. "What do you think?"

"I think Darrin, and Patsy, would have been thrilled."

"She—"

"Didn't make it." He ran his thumb over her hand. "But I saw her before she died. I was able to tell her I was sorry, again."

"It wasn't your fault, Luke. None of it."

"I know that now."

"Would be willing to help me tell the story . . . as my consultant?"

"MacKenzie, you'll also need money—"

"Greg. I will *have* money. Where should we start the bidding for my wedding photos?"

"Wedding—"

She had her gaze on Luke, who didn't blink, his eyes widening. Not unlike the first time he'd seen her walk into the ranger station. Interest, curiosity.

But this time, with a smile toying on his gorgeous face.

"I might be overplaying my role, but if you're willing to go back to LA with me, it's going to mean lights, camera, a world of not hiding in the shadows, but living in the limelight. Are you sure you're ready for that?"

"Are you ready to marry a redneck from the East Hills of Tennessee?"

"Um, I think I'm the real redneck here."

"I'm in a chick flick," Greg said, but grinned at the pair of them.

Luke chuckled and knelt beside the bed. "MacKenzie Grace, superhero, surprise woman who set me free, and keeper of my heart, will you marry me?"

"Yep," she said softly. "On one condition."

"What's that?"

"We get married in Harmony. It's time for my worlds to meet each other."

He nodded, then leaned over the bed to kiss her again. She ran her hand into the rough on his face, pulled him close. "Ready for this?"

"And . . . action."

Epilogue

"FIVE HUNDRED ACTORS MILLING AROUND AND MY REDNECK cousin from the hills gets all the love." Greg's low toned mutter caught Kenzie's ears as she walked through the pressroom, and she had to laugh.

"It's not every day that Hollywood meets a bona-fide hero," she said glancing at Luke, now talking with Chris Hemsworth. The two made an impressive pair, caught in the flash of a nearby camera. "But Luke *is* hoarding the limelight."

Admittedly, even Kenzie had to take a long second look at her husband earlier when she stepped out of the bedroom this afternoon and spotted him at the bottom of the stairs wearing an Armani tux, his blond hair pulled back into a tidy bun, very metro-chic, much to his dismay.

His protests stopped just long enough for him to press his hands to his heart and generate a starlit smile at her gold, diamond-beaded Valentino creation.

"I should go back into hiding," he said, pressing a kiss to her cheek after she came down the stairs. "I'm just a scruffy *nerfherder* from the woods."

"*My* scruffy nerfherder," she said as she curled a gloved hand around his neck and kissed his lips. "I like that you've caught up on your Star Wars."

"Which makes me ask—why can't I wear a pair of clean jeans and a dress shirt?" He jutted out his arm for her to take as they walked out to the hired limo.

"Because your superstar wife just might take the stage tonight and nab her very first Oscar, and when she does the camera will pan to you. You don't want to look like something she dragged in from the woods," Greg said, opening the door.

"But I *am* something she dragged in from the woods," he said.

"No. You're the consultant on her next project."

"And excellent eye candy," Kenzie said, which only sent the scowl farther across Luke's face.

"You look beautiful, honey." Her mother stood beside Greg, styled and dressed in a bedazzled sleeveless black Chanel gown that Kenzie ordered had custom made. No borrowing for her mother—this dress she'd take back home to Harmony. Would probably wear it to church occasionally.

"So do you, Mama." Kenzie leaned down and kissed her mother's cheek.

Her father stood next to her mom dressed in a tux. He beamed at her, his graying hair freshly cut, grinning. "I'm so proud of you."

"I've already won because you're here."

It never felt more true as she introduced them to the red carpet, the fans, and seen her parents' expressions at meeting movie stars they'd only seen on the big screen.

She'd tried to talk them into moving to LA, but they preferred their simpler life in Harmony, the cute bungalow she'd purchased for them within walking distance to church and Daddy's job at the school, which he insisted on keeping.

Apparently, LA wasn't their kind of life. A sentiment shared by her new husband who'd acted like he might be choking under the smog and bustle of the city. She'd finally rescued him by getting him a job on her shoot, filling in as a military and arms consultant for her Hayes O'Brien 006 character.

A job that he'd easily manhandled into his own, of course. Suddenly Hollywood had an easily accessible real life special ops soldier in their midst.

Which meant Kenzie finally felt like she'd nailed the role with some authenticity. More, her new credit as associate producer had netted her shares, projected income, and influence with backers who had gladly put up money for her indie film.

Which won its first award at Cannes. Then Toronto, the Sundance, and finally, tonight in LA.

Kenzie still glowed with the heat of the applause. And not one, but two Oscars, one for best actress in an indie film, also.

And when she took the stage, she looked right at her parents and thanked them. Applauding them.

Setting it all right in her heart.

Afterwards, in the post-ceremony photos, she's raised the statuettes above her head in triumph—heavy as they were— as the cameras flashed and allowed herself a small, "Ooh-rah."

Luke had stood back, his grin all the award she really needed.

Now, she simply wanted to get out of the line of reporters who—yes, wanted her words about the Oscars, but seemed just as interested in her new husband.

She reached for Luke's arm as they stood in line to chat with Michael and Kelly. And after them, Kenzie spotted Twila from *Hollywood Today*. Wouldn't you know it, Twila had cornered Nils, chatting him up about his recent superhero movie.

It was the perfect role for him—spandex and body-shaping garments.

She noticed he came without a date this year.

The thought carried her through the interview with Kelly and Michael, even made her grin as Luke and Michael Strahan compared guns. No body-shaping attire needed for Luke—he filled out his tux without any help.

"I like them," he said as he followed her to the next interview line. "He used to be a football player."

"See, you don't have to give up your man card when you move to Hollywood."

"It's not the man card I'm worried about. It's choking to death with the loss of clean air and sunlight."

"Does my redneck need a trip out to Tennessee soon?"

Luke nodded, his smile dimming. "I need to stop in and see Pop too."

The thought of his father, fading too quickly back in Tennessee made her squeeze his arm. "We'll be filming there for two months starting in a couple weeks. And then after the movie is in the can, maybe we take some time off."

"Go back and live in the cabin for a while?" Luke said as the line thinned.

"Don't you mean vacation home?"

But he wasn't looking at her. And, from his darkened expression, the grim set of his jaw, something wasn't right. She'd seen that look before, and for a second, she harkened back nearly nine months.

For once in your life, Kenzie, do what you're told.

She stiffened, and felt his hand touch the small of her back. His voice, quick and sharp in her ear. "Stay here."

She turned in time to see him intercept . . . Nils? What—? With a hand to his chest.

Nils pulled out a gift bag, his gaze fixed on Kenzie. His words floated to her. "But it's our tradition."

"Not anymore." This from Luke, who also glanced at Kenzie. "Not when you humiliated her, and broke her heart. Keep walking, Nils."

Looking at Luke she realized, *yes*, she'd found it. The difference between acting and the real thing.

She didn't have to win an award to know that spending her life with Luke would be the one role that gave her life meaning. Impact.

Joy.

And, right where she belonged.

She felt Greg's hand on her back, guiding her toward the *Hollywood Tonight* crowd. "Be nice," he whispered into her ear. She hid a scowl. But the magazine had paid enough for her wedding photos to help get her to Cannes, which landed her first distribution deal, so she pasted on a smile.

Twila held the mic to her. "What a whirlwind year it's been for you, MacKenzie. Last year at this time, you'd been attacked by a stalker. This year you showed up with two Oscars, and a husband." Twila glanced at Luke. "Is it true you were a forest ranger?"

Luke had joined them again, Nils neatly dispatched. Now he gave a tight nod. Yes, he definitely wanted to get out of that tux, given the grim expression. His encounter with Nils had clearly snuffed out his good humor.

"So, Luke. How does it feel to be married to a big star, now that she's won two Oscars?"

She held her breath. Because yes, while he seemed to adjust well to Hollywood life, too often she sensed a restlessness just under his skin, a haunted, cornered expression.

What if he said it was too much—all this attention, the whirlwind schedules, the expectations and tabloids and—

151

She hadn't realized how much she longed to hear his answer, the real one, in his heart.

He glanced at Kenzie, and a lazy, sweet smile climbed up his face. "She doesn't have to be a star to turn my world from darkness to light." Then he leaned down, swept his arm around Kenzie, and dipped her with a kiss.

Cameras flashed.

She let out a breath. "Really?" She wanted to cup his face in her hands, but they held her statuettes, so she met his eyes, held his gaze, put all her emotion, raw and fragile in them.

His gaze fixed on hers, unmoving, a warmth there that could stop her heart. "There's nowhere I'd rather be than with you, wherever we are."

Then he kissed her again and she was no longer MacKenzie Grace, but Kenzie Talmadge Alexander, girl from the hills, caught in the arms of her hero.

"Now who's hoarding the limelight?" he said into her ear. She laughed as he righted her.

But Shelly was staring at her dress. "Was that—wait, are you wearing Converse tennis shoes under your dress?"

Kenzie glanced at Greg, winked. What he didn't know . . .

She handed a statuette to Luke, then lifted her hem, showing off her red Converse tennis shoes, appropriately bedazzled for the Oscars.

More camera shots. *Take that, Best Dressed List.*

Then, she walked back to her parents, standing with Greg, grinning. Looped her arm over her shoulders. "What do you say, Mama, ready to get out of here? I know where we can get us an *almost* down home piece of banana cream paeh."

Luke laughed. "You can take the girl out of the hills, but you can't take the redneck out of the girl. C'mon Hayes, I'll see if I can rustle you up some sweet tea."

And, that, right there, was a wrap.

Thank you for reading *You Don't Have to be a Star*, the final book in my Montana Fire series. I hope you have enjoyed Luke and Kenzie's love story.

Would you like news on upcoming releases, freebies and sneak peeks from Susie May?

Sign up for updates at susanmaywarren.com, or scan the QR code!

Have you read the first three books in the Montana Fire series?

Start with *Where There's Smoke*!

She's a smokejumper afraid of fire...

Kate Burns is a legendary smoke jumper, known for her courage and willingness to risk everything to get the job done. Only she has a secret, one she won't admit to anyone.

He can't forget the love they once shared...

Supervisor Jed Ransom commands the Jude County Smoke Jumpers with a reputation as a calm, level-headed leader. Kate is the only one who's ever gotten under his skin.

They must face the flames together...

A raging wildfire in the mountains of Montana brings Kate and Jed together to train up a new team of jumpers. Suddenly, they must face the past they've been running from and the secrets that keep them apart. When an arsonist goes after their team, Kate and Jed must face their deepest fears— and learn to rely on each other as they fight a blaze that could destroy them all.

In this first book of the Montana Fire: Summer of Fire trilogy, Kate and Jed are about to discover that where there's smoke, there just might be a chance to start again.

Want More Like This?

Meet the Montana Marshalls, a family with Big Dreams, and Big Trouble, under the Big Sky, and cousins to the Minnesota Marshalls!

A cowboy protector. A woman in hiding. Forced proximity might turn friends to sweethearts if a stalker doesn't find them first...

Montana rancher Knox Marshall's danger years are behind him. A former bull-rider, he now runs the Marshall family ranch, raising champion bucking bulls for the

National Professional Bullrider's Expo (NBR-X). Wealth and success are his, and he's not looking for trouble.

But trouble is looking for county music star Kelsey Jones. Onstage, the beautiful rising star of the Yankee Belles becomes the person she longs to be—vivacious and confident—burying the brokenness she carries from a violent assault. But her attacker just might be on the loose...

Knox and Kelsey's paths collide when an explosion at an NBR-X event traps them in the rubble, igniting Knox's obsession to find the bomber and protect Kelsey...no matter the cost.

Start the epic romantic suspense today!

Discover the newest additions to the Marshall Family Saga

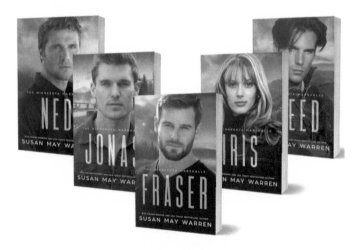

Start your journey with *Fraser*, the firstborn Minnesota Marshall!

Fraser Marshall is pretty sure his career as a Spec Ops fighter is over. Yes, he's gone into private security, working for Jones, Inc, but his last gig ended with him wounded and taken captive. And those wounds just won't heal. The last thing he wants to do is stick around his family's winery pressing grapes. But what choices does he have?

The answer comes via a panicked phone call from his kid brother, Creed.

Help, Fraser. I'm in over my head...

Yeah he is, because he's run away with a princess, with her bodyguard hot on the trail. And said bodyguard, **Pippa Butler** is going to hunt them down, no matter the cost.

Even if she has to join forces with a bossy, arrogant former American SEAL. But Pippa has her own set of lethal skills, and if Fraser gets in the way, she'll leave him on the side of the road. Still, maybe he's not a terrible side-kick. He is handsome, and he makes her laugh...

No, no, bad Pippa! She has no room for a man—an American—in her life. And Fraser hasn't ever considered slowing down. Even if Pippa has him wondering if there is a different future ahead.

But there's more to the story than a Romeo-and-Juliet runaway romance. Princess Imani has seen a murder, and the perpetrator isn't going to let her get away. Will Fraser and Pippa find the couple first?

And if they do, can they work together to keep them safe?

It'll be tough if their hearts get in the way...

Dive into book one of the epic, romantic, globe-trotting suspense of the Minnesota Marshalls!

Available in ebook, print, and audiobook.

Thank you for reading

Thank you so much for reading *You Don't Have to be a Star*. I hope you enjoyed the story. If you did, would you be willing to do me a favor? Head over to the *product page* and leave a review. It doesn't have to be long—just a few words to help other readers know what they're getting. (But no spoilers! We don't want to wreck the fun!)

I'd love to hear from you—not only about this story, but about any characters or stories you'd like to read in the future. Write to me at: susan@susanmaywarren.com. And if you'd like to see what's ahead, stop by www.susanmaywarren.com .

I also have regular updates that contain sneak peeks, reviews, upcoming releases, and free, fun stuff for my reader friends. Sign up on www.susanmaywarren.com or scan my QR code below.

Thank you again for reading!
Susie May

About the Author

With nearly 2 million books sold, critically acclaimed novelist Susan May Warren is the Christy, RITA, and Carol award-winning author of over ninety novels with Tyndale, Barbour, Steeple Hill, and Summerside Press. Known for her compelling plots and unforgettable characters, Susan has written contemporary and historical romances, romantic-suspense, thrillers, rom-com, and Christmas novellas.

With books translated into eight languages, many of her novels have been ECPA and CBA bestsellers, were chosen as Top Picks by *Romantic Times*, and have won the RWA's Inspirational Reader's Choice contest and the American Christian Fiction Writers Book of the Year award. She's a three-time RITA finalist and an eight-time Christy finalist.

Publishers Weekly has written of her books, "Warren lays bare her characters' human frailties, including fear, grief, and resentment, as openly as she details their virtues of love, devotion, and resiliency. She has crafted an engaging tale of romance, rivalry, and the power of forgiveness."

Library Journal adds, "Warren's characters are well-developed and she knows how to create a first rate contemporary romance…"

Susan is also a nationally acclaimed writing coach, teaching at conferences around the nation, and winner of the 2009 American Christian Fiction Writers Mentor of the Year award. She loves to help people launch their writing careers. She is the founder of www.MyBookTherapy.com and www.LearnHowtoWriteaNovel.com, a writing website that helps authors get published and stay published. She is also the author of the popular writing method *The Story Equation.*

Find excerpts, reviews, and a printable list of her novels at www.susanmaywarren.com and connect with her on social media.

facebook.com/susanmaywarrenfiction

instagram.com/susanmaywarren

x.com/susanmaywarren

bookbub.com/authors/susan-may-warren

goodreads.com/susanmaywarren

amazon.com/Susan-May-Warren

Also by Susan May Warren

ALASKA AIR ONE RESCUE

One Last Shot

One Last Chance

One Last Promise

One Last Stand

THE MINNESOTA MARSHALLS

Fraser

Jonas

Ned

Iris

Creed

THE EPIC STORY OF RJ AND YORK

Out of the Night

I Will Find You

No Matter the Cost

THE MONTANA MARSHALLS

Knox

Tate

Ford

Wyatt

Ruby Jane

SKY KING RANCH

Sunrise

Sunburst

Sundown

GLOBAL SEARCH AND RESCUE

The Way of the Brave

The Heart of a Hero

The Price of Valor

MONTANA FIRE

Where There's Smoke (Summer of Fire)

Playing with Fire (Summer of Fire)

Burnin' For You (Summer of Fire)

Oh, The Weather Outside is Frightful (Christmas novella)

I'll be There (Montana Fire/Deep Haven crossover)

Light My Fire (Summer of the Burning Sky)

The Heat is On (Summer of the Burning Sky)

Some Like it Hot (Summer of the Burning Sky)

You Don't Have to Be a Star (Montana Fire spin-off)

MONTANA RESCUE

If Ever I Would Leave You (novella prequel)

Wild Montana Skies

Rescue Me

A Matter of Trust

Crossfire (novella)

Troubled Waters

Storm Front

Wait for Me

THE DEEP HAVEN COLLECTION

Happily Ever After

Tying the Knot

The Perfect Match

My Foolish Heart

The Shadow of your Smile

You Don't Know Me

**A complete list of Susan's novels can be found at
susanmaywarren.com/novels/bibliography/.**

You Don't Have to be a Star
Montana Fire, Book 9
Published by SDG Publishing
Copyright © 2016 by Susan May Warren

This book is a work of fiction. Names, characters, places, and incidents are either products of the author's imagination or used fictitiously. Any similarity to actual people, organizations, and/or events is purely coincidental.

Scripture quotations are taken from the King James Version of the Bible.

Scripture quotations are also taken from the Holy Bible, New International Version®, NIV®. Copyright© 1973, 1978, 1984, 2011 by Biblica, Inc®. Used by permission of Zondervan. All rights reserved worldwide.

For more information about Susan May Warren, please access the author's website at the following address: www.susanmaywarren.com.

Published in the United States of America.